MORTAL MUSINGS

Aria Glazki

ANIKA PRESS

ISBN: 978-1-943572-02-1
Copyright registration number:
TX0008178609

First Edition: August 2015

Forging Forever:

Mending Heartstrings
Tasting Temptation
Taking Chances

Standalone stories:

Fragments That Fit
Summer Seduction
Fallen
The Whedonite
Immortalized in Ink

For all those who feel invisible

Chapter 1

<p>riter's block had walled him in. Again. So much for being a "professional." It wasn't even that there were ideas milling around and he couldn't find the right words. That would have been infinitely better than the void in his mind. So Brett just sat there, squishing a stress ball and staring at a computer-screen rendition of a page, waiting to be filled. Taunting him with its emptiness.

He had nothing left to say.

Well, that wasn't quite true; the standard words were still there. Sinister shadows and scar-faced gangsters wouldn't cut it, though. He needed to find a new way to describe the mysteries of the world, but his normally overflowing well of words had inexplicably run dry, leaving him trapped in its parched depth.

Resolute, Brett set down the tortured stress ball and placed his fingers over the keys. A light breeze ruffled the curtain behind his computer. The cursor blinked almost hypnotically on the page. Still the words didn't come.

Perhaps he had lost his muse. But then, had there ever been a muse guiding him? If there had, wouldn't he have been more of a success? More original in his characterizations and phrasing?

And why would a creature of infinite inspiration even bother with humans rather than frolicking in the fantastic worlds its own imagination and powers could have created?

No, a random thought or word that inspired a masterpiece didn't come from a muse. It sprang from inside the writer—from experience and life, or adoration, however fleeting, of the subject. Brett had always thought so. No, known so. Waiting for inspiration from an outside, mythical source was merely an excuse. People's lives and words, their ideas and feelings inspired the transcendent works of art they produced.

Not today, though. Or for the last few weeks.

Brett puffed his breath out and shook his head in a futile attempt to clear it, leaning back in his chair. If muses did exist—which they *didn't*—they clearly favored people who didn't possess any innate inclinations toward art, since those who did suffered endlessly from writer's block or similar inabilities to produce what was aching to pour out of them, despite being trapped under impenetrable layers of…something.

Brett shut his eyes and massaged his temples. Maybe he should give up for the day, deadline be damned.

Thus from the mires of frustration, yet another blamed her kind for his own shortcomings. How arrogant and vain to believe that muses would favor one human over another. Their purpose was to inspire the creative production of ideas, not to concoct the ideas themselves. It was absurd to expect a muse to do anything at all until an idea had already been uncovered. Such blame and condemnation for a world of which he knew nothing and creatures he could not even begin to fathom! Blame in no sense different than that of every other frustrated artist, coming from yet another one who considered himself elevated beyond the norm. *So* exceptional, though he differed not at all from his predecessors. If only she could show him the error of his ways.

Nearly the entirety of her existence had been filled with the ache of silently guiding others, pouring herself into the work of innumerable mortals—her endless ungrateful charges—and for what? To be sent to yet another one.

Suddenly the writer's fingers began tapping the keys before him.

> Forget your worry and your woes
> Forget your friends, family, and foes
> They do not matter. It is we:
> The muses, elves, and the faerie,
> Who give up everything to you.
>
> We do not ask if it is just;
> We don't complain—we know we must.
> It is our duty to inspire;
> We do not bother to conspire
> Against one or another of all thee.
>
> We slave away for your sake only.
> You do not care if we are lonely,
> Or that we yearn for a place to stay—
> A place to pause from our weary way.
> You just demand the inspiration
>
> Without a single word of thanks.
> And yet we do not play the pranks
> You so believe we're meant to do,
> The ones I wish I could with you,
> For then you'd notice me,

The muse who stands beside your chair.
You never think if I am there
'Xcept when ideas do not flow,
And then you wallow in your woe
And fault poor innocents like me.

Now read these words,
Make my voice heard:
I must not give you any dreams;
I wait like you until one gleams
Yet you blame me.

You cannot see 'til I will it so,
But the Fates won't let you go
On believing not in us,
Who guide you still without a fuss.
Someday your eyes will clear

And you'll see me.

The realization of her words on the screen curved Allie's lips. *How's* that *for inspiration?*

Brett blinked at the words he couldn't remember typing. A poem? He turned slightly, looking first at the curl of hair brushing his shoulder, then to the unfamiliar face beside his.

The stranger who filled his vision paid no attention to him. Her cheeks were flushed. Before Brett could process what he was seeing, she turned away to stalk about the small room. She examined their surroundings unabashedly, scoffing at his possessions as though he himself were inconsequential. Almost as if he wasn't even there.

Had he passed out at the computer? This didn't feel like a

dream, but maybe he'd hit his head on the desk, hard enough to jumble what was left of his mind.

Brett couldn't look away. Such undiluted condescension intrigued him almost as much as the drapes of silken cloth he supposed were a dress, floating about her body like a cloud, though of course that wasn't possible. Then again, was "possible" even a factor in what he was seeing? The nearly transparent, grayish-white material shifted as she moved, exposing tantalizing glimpses of her flesh to his curious eyes, but she didn't notice him staring.

Similar clouds must have filled his brain, since he hadn't even wondered yet how she'd gotten into his house—*into his office!*—without him noticing. Maybe she was a friend of his sister's, playing some poorly planned prank? Or maybe hours of staring fruitlessly at the blankness had caused him to hallucinate, and neither the strange words nor the girl were actually there.

Brett's lips pulled into a humorless smile. Maybe *this* was his muse, sent as a joke by whichever powers that be as a response to his mental ranting.

What a completely idiotic idea, especially since muses were supposed to be invisible. *And not real,* he reminded himself yet again.

Nonplussed by the creature before him, who still hadn't acknowledged his presence, Brett glanced back at the text on his computer. Muses? Ones who were mad and believed humans to be ungrateful? *Right.* Maybe she was a witch who had enchanted him to write these words and hadn't realized the spell had broken when she had stopped coming up with new ones.

Or maybe it was time to stop making up stories, even though that was all he'd wanted to do for the preceding hours, and go get checked out. Muses? Or even better, witches??

"They don't exist, Brett," he muttered under his breath.

She spun toward him at his words, but even then her attitude didn't change. After the briefest glance at him, she continued her exploration of his ancient trophies and posters, and other knick-knacks leftover from his college years.

Finally inspiration struck, though of course not in any way that would translate into a sellable book. It wasn't as though she wasn't aware of him. No, more like she thought he couldn't see *her*. Which made even less sense, but felt true, for whatever the hell that was worth.

She didn't touch anything, as if afraid of making noise and attracting his attention. A quiet grace filled her movements despite the anger in her clenched fists and jaw. Anger at him? What could he have possibly done to offend her? She was in *his* house!

Having examined all of the useless possessions in sight, Allie returned her focus to her charge. Who was staring at her. She glanced briefly behind herself though his gaze was nearly palpable, boring into her. Except he could not see her!

No mortal could.

Nevertheless, she did feel steeped in an odd heaviness that affected each of her movements. And he was unquestionably looking at her. Was she being penalized for her rash behavior? Causing him to write her words was indeed against the rules, but it should not have resulted in this! The fabled race was, after all, what he himself had been contemplating. Moreover, if she *were* to be punished, revealing her to a charge wasn't likely to be the penalty.

Still he continued to stare at her. Worse, his eyes drifted lower, lingering over her form for some unknown reason. Allie glanced down at herself as a gust of wind blew through the slightly opened window. Her kind didn't much worry about nudity, but humans were obsessed with physicality. Not that she resembled current mortal standards for sensuality and attractiveness. Contrary to contemporary misconceptions, muses were not all slim and flawlessly shaped, though their attire was intended to be incomparably free, fashioned from clouds. Magic kept them in place, but her previously flattering covering had nearly dissipated.

Startled, Allie managed only to snatch the tattered blanket she had previously noticed on his couch and hold it in front of her progressively exposed body as the last wisps vanished.

This was outside the bounds of even Brett's imagination. His unexpected visitor stood suddenly naked before him. Embarrassment flushed the face that had so recently been filled with contempt. Only the throw she had snatched covered her, draping from her fists to the floor but still revealing the outside curves of her breasts and the slopes of her hips. He could have sworn she'd been dressed a minute ago. Then again, she hadn't been there at all moments before that, so what did he know?

Slowly, his eyes trailed down and up her body again as Brett willed her to disappear the same way her clothing had, to become nothing more than an odd dream, or perhaps his inspiration to move past his writer's block. But unless he was vividly hallucinating, there was no denying the woman standing before him. Naked.

Brett cleared his throat and started to unbutton his shirt so she could cover up. Tempting as her revealed body was, it wasn't helping whatever was going on. Her already pale skin drained of color. Her chin notched up, though she couldn't prevent a step back. Clearly, she was in need of medical attention, especially if she thought breaking into his home and exposing her body would result in sexual advances on his end.

He'd get her reasonably covered and then call Wes—an orderly at the Lyssa Iasso Psychiatric Center, who'd helped Brett with some research for his last book. Then he could get back to work, if that was what staring at a blank screen could be called. Maybe he'd file a police report, just in case. *Not* to procrastinate.

Allie fought not to back away from the presumptuous charge who was stripping off his garb. Apparently her vulnerable nudity was all that was required to inspire his desire for the sweaty mortal copulation her previous charges had occasionally attempted to venerate in their work. Perhaps she shouldn't have been surprised. Humans took everything else she and her kind had to offer for granted—why not her body, now that one of them could see it? How exactly that had become the case still wasn't clear, and wishing she could revert to her true form wasn't having the desired effect.

She was supposed to have control over who could see her! That may have changed, but her mastery over her own body unequivocally would not. She strained to reign in her frustrations and the gathering tears. She had to figure out what had trapped her in this realm, and until she did, she apparently had no hope of returning to her true form, or to faerie. Would she be able to reverse whatever had happened?

When the writer stretched out the man-made garment in her direction, Allie could no longer resist backing away, which effectively blocked her between him, his couch, and the cabinet wedged into the corner. She resolutely forced herself to breathe, relying on ingrained stubbornness to maintain an outward appearance of relative calm.

Chapter 2

When the redhead didn't take his shirt, Brett stepped forward to drape it over her shoulders. A sharp intake of breath accompanied his movement, and fear flooded her expression for an instant. *Good.* At least she was with it enough to understand her presence wasn't welcome, not that he was a physical threat to her. Not loving the idea, he nonetheless turned his back so she could button the shirt. His treacherous mind pictured the blanket slipping away from her body.

Brett clenched his jaw and pulled out his cell phone so he could call the nice men in white jackets to cart her away.

She hadn't yet said a word, so Brett nearly jumped when she spoke. "Thank you." Her voice was oddly melodic, like the lush lower tones of a violin. He turned back around to face her. She had moved away from the corner. If she was trying to escape, maybe she had a better understanding of what was happening than he'd thought. Then again, he didn't really have a solid grasp of the last few minutes, so who was he to judge?

They watched each other, both obviously wary. Brett's eyes drifted from her lightly twitching lips to the edge of his shirt that now grazed the tops of her thighs.

This wasn't right. Either she was insane, and lost, in which case the direction his mind had taken would be grossly inappropriate and somewhat predatory, or she was a burglar. Not that he had anything to steal. Crazy made more sense. She didn't seem threatening, other than the potentially explosive danger of insanity.

"Seeking inspiration?" The acerbic words snapped his eyes back to her face. Gone was the timidity of a minute ago. Now her eyes had narrowed, and her lips pressed unabashedly together in derision.

Brett almost apologized. Until he remembered that *she* was the intruder in this scenario. He crossed his arms to seem appropriately intimidating in case she was nothing more than a clumsy thief. Who worked naked.

Allie's gaze jumped to the bunched muscles in the writer's folded arms, then to the defined planes of his torso, only thinly veiled by tight, white cloth. He clearly took care of his body, unlike many of her previous charges. Perhaps he was accustomed to mortal women falling at his feet at the merest glance. Was he expecting her to do the same?

It was unthinkable, though she probably should have avoided challenging him. Occasionally, she had been unable to hold back her temper with the other fae, but those moments were rare, particularly because she spent little time around her peers. Solitude was not an option now, however, since the sole clues to her inexplicable transformation lay in this room, with this charge. She could not risk him involving this realm's authorities if she had any hope of returning home.

With his arms clenched over his chest and the alert focus in his eyes, he looked downright menacing—nothing at all like he had seemed when she had arrived.

"How did you get in here?"

She should have expected the steel in his voice. From his perspective, she had invaded his space. Ironically, it had been his silent pleas for inspiration that had caused him to be assigned as her next charge, leading to her current predicament. "The answer is within you. I cannot provide it for you."

He crooked an eyebrow.

If only she could use different words, but she was forbidden to tell anything directly to her assignments. Her sole role was to inspire those already on the right track.

"Don't play games with me," he snapped. "I don't make a habit of placating or welcoming criminals. I should just call the police and have them handle you. Or do you get your kicks by being arrested for breaking and entering?"

Those cursed tears were making progress, prickling along her eyes.

He dropped his tone to a threatening whisper, deliberately punctuating his words. "How. Did you. Get in here?"

Allie scrambled for a way to explain the inexplicable—to convince him of a reality she could not state and in which he did not believe regardless. A golden glimmer above his shoulder drew her gaze. Sprite's dust sprinkled over his head. Or was that merely wishful thinking? She seized the glimmer of hope to send the writer a burst of inspiration.

He slipped the contraption he held back into his pocket, but otherwise there was no sign that her powers had taken effect. Worse, her attempt had drained the few remnants of her magic. Faerie was lost to her now.

✧ ✧ ✧

The intruder's leaf-green eyes closed, pain echoing in the lines of her expression. No matter how much he tried to remind himself *she* was the interloper, Brett felt like a bully. Deeply red hair curled over his shirt, which now covered her almost pearlescent skin. Skin so purely white had clearly never been touched by the sun. *Exactly*, his mind whispered. *Because she's not human.*

Maybe she really was a fairy. The thought sparked others in his idea-starved mind. Not a fairy—a muse. His muse, transformed into physical form.

Not back to that, again.

Absurd. He should read less folklore, no matter how fascinating it was. There was no way a muse had appeared beside him, typed bizarre words on his computer, and then taken mortal form in vanishing clothing. He should just call…someone. The plan was fuzzy now. Was he losing his mind?

"Who are you?" he asked.

Her eyes snapped open, but the misery was still evident in the inward slant of her brows. Her earlier contempt, however, had completely disappeared. Nearly perfectly pink lips parted without sound at his question. Tears reflected the exquisite color of her eyes, but she blinked them back. "I am not certain," she finally murmured.

She sank fluidly to the couch behind her. Despair hunched her shoulders and bowed her head. Her hands rested listlessly beside her knees.

Help her, an unknown voice in his mind whispered. He wanted to protect her, this unexplained visitor who looked so lost, and innocent.

Innocent? Hadn't she broken into his home?

Maybe she'd been intended as a distraction, a decoy while others pilfered the sparse offerings of the other rooms. But there were better ways to distract a man than this broken vulnerability, and what he'd seen of her body was perfectly suited to every one that came to mind.

Against all reason, he felt the urge to comfort her, to stroke her hair. Her beautifully silken hair that reminded him of sunlight glinting through garnets. Some vestige of logic stopped him from approaching her while she was so scantily dressed.

Brett cleared his throat. "I'll get you some clothes."

She didn't react.

He glanced at his computer then headed out of the office, leaving the door wide open, just in case.

Allie didn't move after the writer left. If she was no longer a member of faerie, she was essentially nobody. The pain of the loss was incomparable to anything she had experienced. She had never quite fit in with her peers, but she had also never considered abandoning everything she had known. Some ancient stories spoke of muses who had preferred the mortal realm, sacrificing their identities, their very essence, to join it. In every instance she could remember, however, those muses had chosen their own paths, while hers had, inexplicably, been selected for her.

She strained to breathe through her gathering tears but couldn't fight them all. Droplets coursed down her cheeks. She didn't bother to wipe them away until a shadow appeared on the floor. Allie swiped at her face before looking at her former charge. She had to stop crying. Somehow, she would find her way back. She may not always be fond of her role, but she certainly wasn't destined to be trapped in the dingy den of this human!

He set the items he held onto the couch beside her then resumed his initial position in the desk chair. A few taps later, the screen became black. He swiveled in his chair.

"You should put those on." He laced his fingers casually in his lap.

She brushed her hand over the mortal clothing. His? Perhaps he had a woman in his life. This entire situation could be even more complex than she had previously realized, though his living arrangement wasn't her primary concern. Allie steeled herself to ask the question she wasn't certain she wanted answered. "Do you…" She swallowed. "Do you plan to summon the police?"

Crinkles appeared on his forehead, and a blankness filled his eyes before he gently shook his head. Perhaps the golden dusting she had seen hadn't been a desperate wish, but a fortuitously timed layer of protection! Sprites could sense other creatures of faerie, so it was possible one had decided to intervene on Allie's behalf when her own power had flickered out. If she ever returned to faerie, she would have to find and thank the benevolent being. At least for the moment, the writer didn't appear inclined to throw her to the mercy of other mortals.

"I guess, I'd like an explanation," he finally answered.

"An explanation." Allie sighed, licking her bottom lip before catching it between her teeth. When she noticed the surfacing of the nervous habit, she exhaled again. "All of the answers are within you, like the words you write and ideas you have—all there, waiting to be discovered and accepted."

He stilled. "What do you know about my writing?"

"Only that you write." Past particulars weren't necessary for her role. Muses did learn about their charges as they worked, but she hadn't been his long enough to glean much. "Do you not?" She had never encountered a writer who wasn't proud to be recognized as such.

He stood without responding, although, she hadn't truly been asking. Silence suffused the room once more. Allie refused to avert her gaze, focusing instead on various elements of his appearance: hazel eyes with elusive specks of gold, though she may have imagined those; slightly ragged hair which undoubtedly fell prey to the frustrated tugging of his fingers; lightly tanned skin, set off by the white of his garb; and remarkably clean, bare feet.

"Are you hungry?" The question ended her somewhat calming examination.

"I don't know," she answered idiotically. The question itself was an astonishing sign of hospitality, though not if the sprite's dust had indeed dissuaded the writer from more practical action. How long would the magical interference protect her?

In truth, she wouldn't have been opposed to consuming something, but she did not in fact know whether there was anything edible in the mortal world. Humans often partook of some manner of sustenance as they worked, but everything she had seen had come packaged in one little bag or another and certainly did not appear appetizing. It had been nothing like the nourishment of the fae, all of which was extraordinarily fresh and flowed with life-sustaining energy.

His eyes narrowed again. She was beginning to recognize that as a sign of his distrust. "Right. Well, I'll go make something." He stalled in the doorway, adding, "You should put the clothes on. Kitchen's down the hall."

Once he had gone, Allie allowed herself to examine the items he had brought. On the plus side, it was obvious what was worn where: a short, loose pair of bottoms, and a purple top without sleeves. The items appeared too small to be the writer's. Hopefully the garments' owner wouldn't be opposed to her donning them. She slipped on the pieces, though they felt rough and scratchy against her skin, then picked up the garment he had originally given her and ventured after him.

Though she had spent hundreds of years with charges in the mortal realm, she had rarely seen anything other than their workspaces. Occasionally, some charges would enjoy working outside, so she could pass her time in parks or forests. Apparently this was not the case this time. His workspace was enclosed, dingy, and darkened by the heavy fabric that mostly obscured the partially opened window.

The last thing she expected to encounter beyond the door was an open, airy room filled with sunshine streaming happily through the angled windows that dominated the opposite wall. Decorative curtains surrounded the windows but left them bare, welcoming the light that glanced off a glass table that stood in front of a large couch. Allie paused, trying to understand why he would bar himself from the outside world as he worked but embrace it in the rest of his home. Had the homes of all her charges differed so extremely from their workspaces? Surely not.

"In here!" the writer called, withdrawing her from her contemplation. Allie obediently moved toward his voice. She was in no position to reject his hospitality. Regardless of how drastically mortal food differed from that of the fae, not eating for the unknown duration of her entrapment in this realm would be foolish.

The kitchen, too, was lighter and more welcoming than his workspace. There, his hair had seemed as dingy as the room itself—a plain, almost unwashed brown—whereas now, sunlight picked out more variations in the color, dancing through his hair as both he and the rays of light moved.

That same light glinted off the large blade that moved ceaselessly yet deftly in his hand. Bloody scenes from twisted works, the creation of which she had had the misfortune of overseeing, raced through her mind. Allie moved no farther than the entry-way.

The thumping of the blade's glancing blows against the board below dominated her thoughts until a sizzling harmonized with it. A pleasant smell reached her, and Allie instructed herself to ignore the potential danger until it was a more definitive, immediate threat. The blade continued its menacing beat. Allie's nails bit into her palms. She would simply have to keep her temper tightly reigned in and be as pleasant and soothing as possible.

Brett had finished chopping the cucumbers and was about to go searching for his unexpected guest when she spoke from behind him.

"You have a beautiful home."

He busied himself with flipping the chicken thighs in the skillet before reacting. The house had been left to him by his grandparents, and he'd mostly left the living room and kitchen alone, allowing the space to keep the few pleasant memories he had from his adolescence.

"Thanks," he finally answered. Satisfied that the chicken was browning nicely, he wiped his hands on a towel and turned around. She wasn't likely to be a thief, he'd decided, since she'd had ample opportunity simply to walk out his front door. It didn't mean she wasn't a potential danger to him, just that she was insane, or an amnesiac who...

Brett blinked several times as his mind registered her in this new outfit. Vicky's clothes had always been casually appropri-ate—he'd made sure of that—but they looked downright erotic on his guest. The drawstring shorts that hung loosely off his sister's frame clung to the redhead's hips, though not as blatantly as the tank top clung to her upper body. The slight vee revealed more than enough to tantalize any straight man as the fabric stretched over her full breasts, fighting to keep them contained despite her lack of a bra. *She also isn't wearing underwear,* he remembered unhelpfully. His mind flashed to the cartoon cliché of a man's jaw dropping to the ground. The ridiculousness of the image thankfully snapped him out of his near trance.

Unlike when he'd removed his shirt, she seemed unaffected by his staring. Brett still turned away to finish assembling the salad and calm his vastly inappropriate thoughts. He dumped the cucumbers over the lettuce and tomatoes already in his grandmother's favorite salad bowl and reached for the creamy ranch beside it, squirting it over everything before his brain caught up. *Damn it.* "I forgot to ask if you like dressing," he half apologized. Then again, he was being astoundingly hospitable, all things considered.

"I'm certain whatever you are preparing will be wonderful," she answered, her voice pitched higher than before. Apparently she didn't want to make waves, which was actually just fine.

Still, he felt obliged to ask, "You're not a vegetarian, are you?"

She didn't answer. Brett looked to her as he shifted the salad to the island that slanted diagonally across his combination kitchen-dining room. His eyebrows shot up.

"I…don't know?" Her own eyebrows raised slightly over rounded eyes.

Brett didn't press the issue. Worst-case scenario, she'd remember the answer in a few minutes. He checked the chicken again before pulling out place settings. "So do you have a name?"

He busied himself with arranging everything on the mahogany dining table so he could avoid the temptation of looking at her.

"Alexandra." She pronounced it without the short *a* sounds of American English—*Ah-leh-kzahn-drah*. Her gaze caught him when he headed back toward the stove. She still stood in the entryway, holding the shirt he'd taken off earlier. "And yours?"

Well, at least she probably wasn't a stalker. Or she knew to pretend. "Brett." He gestured to the shirt. "You can toss that anywhere. If you're not cold, I mean." Maybe she'd use it to cover up.

She draped it silently on one of the barstools beside the island. Brett tore his eyes away so the chicken wouldn't burn. He brought down a platter and plated the thighs. Somehow, he wasn't surprised that she hadn't made a move toward the table. He gestured toward one of the chairs with his free hand before setting down the steaming chicken. "Please." When in doubt, courtesy had to be the way to go.

Her lips twitched into an uncomfortable smile, but she did walk toward the table. Brett pulled a bottle of wine and some juice from the refrigerator before joining her. When she made no move toward the food, he poured her some wine. Definitely couldn't hurt.

Chapter 3

Allie took the glass from Brett's proffered hand. The settings he had placed at the table left them seated perpendicularly to each other. He watched her with the same intense gaze he had been directing her way since she had entered the kitchen. Entirely unused to this amount of attention, she concentrated instead on the mystery liquid. The pale yellow color wasn't repellent, but she still sniffed it surreptitiously before daring to take a sip. The smooth, slightly tangy taste drew a hum of appreciation from her.

Brett smiled for the first time since her arrival and filled his own glass, then took a sip. When Allie didn't move, he spooned some greens covered in a white goop onto her plate and lifted the platter with meat, holding it for her. Allie picked up the fork beside her plate and selected a small piece. "Thank you."

He nodded slightly in response then served himself. When he didn't begin eating, Allie speared some greens. This level of courtesy was wholly unexpected for her, particularly from a charge. Former charge? The rules of their relationship had undoubtedly been altered, though to what remained a mystery.

Allie distracted herself by trying the mortal food. Fresh juices flowed over her tongue, mingling with a few different shades of flavors. She tried a red piece next, which was different but offered many of the same tastes—presumably from the white goop.

Brett followed her lead and picked up his utensils, though he cut directly into the meat. Allie sipped her drink instead, despite the appetizing scent. She had been pleasantly surprised thus far, but she had no desire to tempt the Fates. Brett's professionally necessary ability to observe derailed that plan.

"You don't like chicken?" he asked, setting down his utensils.

"I have never tasted it before," she answered honestly.

Little lines appeared between his eyebrows. He diverted his gaze and reached for his own glass. "Now's as good a time as any."

Allie steeled herself and cut off a piece of the meat—chicken. What was that mortal cliché? When in Rome…? Hiding a sigh, she resolutely placed the chicken in her mouth. New flavors played over her taste buds: tart, salty, and with a hint of sweetness. She swallowed and eagerly sliced off another piece.

Brett's lips pulled to one side. "Not too bad, right?"

"It's wonderful." She sipped from her glass then ventured to ask, "Where did you learn how to prepare food so well?" Among the fae, everyone had their particular talents and roles; no one switched or acquired an additional skill. As far as she knew, the mortal realm mimicked such specialization. She certainly had never seen any of her charges prepare meals.

"I used to work as a fry cook." His attention returned to his own plate, but her curiosity wasn't sated.

"In order to learn?"

He slanted a look her way as he swallowed. "We needed the money."

"Oh." She nodded as though that response told her everything. She knew mortals exchanged currency, in a variety of forms, for goods, but he appeared to be fairly young. And prior to adulthood, didn't human parents provide for their offspring's needs, including financially? Centuries ago, humans would serve as apprentices at younger ages, though they had rarely switched to an alternate profession afterward.

"It did teach me my way around a kitchen, though," he added.

Allie slipped more chicken into her mouth so chewing would allow her not to respond, if only temporarily. A shadow flew past the windows to her right, drawing Brett's attention.

"Blue jay," he commented, moving another piece of chicken onto his plate.

"Why do you barricade yourself from nature in your workspace?" Allie asked without thinking.

"What do you mean?"

"You would write more easily if you let nature in where you worked, as you do elsewhere in your home. Sunlight streaming through the windows, birds or butterflies flitting past… Nature is pure inspiration. How much closer could one be to ultimate motivation than your natural world—the ideas that created it? You may even be able to eliminate bouts of what you call 'writer's block' altogether."

Brett watched her with eyes narrowed once more. All of the humor and calm of the past few minutes had been wiped from his face. "You're uncertain of who you are. You didn't know whether you eat meat. But you seem to know all about my writing. Why is that?"

Thank whatever power had ensured his large knife was far away, not that he couldn't reach it in less than a few steps. Allie bit her lip, considering her options.

Brett set down his silverware and straightened from the table. Alexandra had frozen, other than the lip that was slowly slipping out from between her teeth. She didn't even seem to be breathing. Then a puff of air escaped along with her bottom lip, reddened by the pressure of her bite. He almost forgot his question. He had to get his mind out of the gutter, or the bedroom, as the case may be.

Lucky for him, Alexandra decided to answer. "It's a part of who I…was."

Brett reached for his wine glass with deceptive calm. There was something she deliberately wasn't saying, almost like she was waiting for him to ask the right question. "Who's that?"

"I was… I worked with artists, writers, musicians, and the like. I helped them tap into their ideas and transform them into reality."

A career counselor of sorts? How could she remember who she had been but claim not to know who she was? Of course, being delusional would pretty much explain it all.

"Nature frequently helps. Helped," she finished.

Brett didn't know what to say. He wasn't even sure why she was still there. Hadn't he had a plan for getting her out of his house? The more he was near her, the less he wanted her to leave. He topped off both their wine glasses instead of saying anything.

He definitely didn't want to think about his writer's block. He didn't want to think at all. Thinking was what kept him from pulling her from her chair and tasting the lips she wouldn't leave alone. If that rose color had been the result of lipstick, she would have nibbled it all off by now.

He replaced the wine bottle less gently than he'd intended. She almost jumped. Brett stabbed some salad onto his fork and bit sharply into the crisp vegetables as if they could satiate him. Alexandra slowly slid a slice of cucumber onto her fork then lifted it in a smooth yet subtle motion to her mouth, as if afraid to draw attention to herself. Brett almost snapped at her to just eat it already, but a drop of dressing plopped onto her lower lip. Her tongue flicked out, covering the droplet and retreating slowly, which left her lip glistening.

Brett grabbed his wine glass and drained it. When he returned it to the table, his eyes fell to his grandma's plate. She had loved the delicate ivy pattern that hugged the rim. And she would have crushed him with the disappointed downward tilt of her mouth for being rude to a guest, even an uninvited one. Especially one who seemed to need help. He had to change the topic.

"Would you like some more salad?" Small talk had to be a safe bet.

She shook her head. Brett picked up his fork but waited until she continued eating before stabbing another piece of lettuce himself.

They emptied both their plates in silence, though Alexandra grew progressively less hesitant as she consumed more wine. Between the two of them, they'd killed the bottle, though he'd definitely had more than her. And her glass was still half full. Apparently she was a lightweight.

Small pink circles had appeared at the tops of her cheeks, and the nervous tension that had been vibrating through her had disappeared. Not a bad change.

Brett stood to clear the plates.

"May I help you clean up?"

It took him a moment to register the question. What was wrong with him? He picked up the empty plates to walk them over to the sink. "You could take the leftovers to the island."

The salad bowl and platter scraped softly against the table as she lifted them. Brett sprayed the other dishes with water before getting out some fridge-friendly glassware. She returned for the wine glasses as he dealt with the leftovers. When he'd turned from putting everything in the fridge, she'd already added the platter and salad bowl to the sink. The silent ease of their movements felt unbelievably comfortable. He gestured to the barstools and waited as she stepped away from the sink with her unfinished wine.

The dishes would have taken him no time at all, but then Alexandra started humming quietly, in a breathless, not-quite-singing sort of way. Brett's movements slowed to match the sweetly soothing melody.

He shut off the water to collect her glass. She read his intentions and slid off the stool with it in hand, but mistimed the motion, bumping into him. He steadied her automatically, hands briefly coming to her wrist and ribcage. He worked the glass from her fingers and set it back on the island.

Her eyes watched him with a mixture of curiosity and innocence. Her mouth was inches from his. Her ribcage expanded unevenly beneath his lingering palm. She'd stopped humming, and her lips were slightly parted.

Brett brushed a loose strand of hair back behind her ear, marveling at its softness. How different she seemed now than when he'd first seen her. Had that been only hours ago?

Different, because of the alcohol. He swallowed the massive lump in his throat he knew wasn't really there and stepped back. "You should get some sleep." Whatever had happened, was happening, they could figure it out in the clarity of morning.

Rizen wasn't happy. Officially, he was merely doing his duty. Unofficially, Matera had given him specific directions tonight. He should have started with Alexandra. He wouldn't have minded watching her body find its way into the arms of sleep. Instead, he sat on the top of a dusty shelf, waiting until the mortal fell asleep, all to run an errand that was, strictly speaking, against the rules.

Dream weavers were frequently sent to help control dreams, of course, allowing mortal minds to process what would otherwise drive them to insanity if given free reign. But they could do more than that.

In that vulnerable state, humans had no defenses against weavers' powers. Against him. None, other than the rules enforced by the Fates and the guiding powers. Including Matera, usually.

"Exceptional circumstances," she had claimed, as if one impulsive muse deserved the leniency he'd been denied.

Rizen didn't envy Alexandra, of course, trapped among the mortals. And he'd broken the rules before. That was why Matera had sent for him, not that she'd admitted it. He'd been younger then. Young, and green, and stupid. And infatuated with a dream he'd helped create.

He knew better now: he hated everything.

He did his job, and he ate well, and slept on the softest clouds, and watched nymphs and muses bathing when they didn't think anyone was there. It wasn't a pretty existence, but pretty was overrated.

Rizen kicked his feet impatiently, accidentally striking his heel against some book. The writer opened his eyes and sat up slightly, looking around for the source of the noise. Not that he could see the weaver. But Rizen's radiating pain wouldn't make the ridiculous wait any more pleasant.

Then again, if he was breaking one rule, he could break another. Rizen popped from the top of the shelf to the couch and dug into the pouch around his waist. His breath puffed the sleeping dust into the air. Missing another hour of imagining Alexandra naked wouldn't irreparably harm the human. It *would* save Rizen some time.

He waited a few minutes while the human sank deeper into sleep then concocted a song with Matera's message, which the writer wouldn't actively remember. He'd simply no longer think Alexandra was insane or a threat. It wouldn't be much help to the former muse, but anything more would be too noticeable a shift in his attitude. No one could know Rizen had interfered.

Satisfied that the impression had taken hold, Rizen popped to the other room. Alexandra slept calmly, half-covered by the blankets. Unfortunately, she was dressed. Rizen stood beside her on the bed and reached his hand out over her body, yearning for the touch. Outside her dreams, she wouldn't feel anything he did. But then, neither would he.

Rizen dropped his hand and sat down on the mounded blanket to focus. He built a dream, crafting a garden with an idyllic white gazebo, then pulled her in. Her mind dressed her automatically in clouds, as though she were still a muse. Water droplets sparkled on her skin, enhancing the illusion of the design. She spun slowly within the small gazebo, searching for the power behind the shift into the dream. Rizen sat on the wall. His heart pounded ferociously.

"Hello, Alexandra," he said with feigned calm when she faced him. Showing himself to mortals was against the rules, but Alexandra wasn't truly mortal. It had been more centuries than he wanted to count since anyone other than the guiding powers had seen him—his punishment for interfering in a human's life.

"You're a weaver, but I don't know you," Alexandra stated simply.

"You know all weavers, do you?"

Most, she thought, not knowing that he could hear her. "Is this a mortal dream?" she asked aloud.

"In the flesh." He laughed bitterly at his own, private joke.

She gazed outside the gazebo, at the garden he'd created. "It's beautiful."

"More pleasant to look at than a weaver, then?" he challenged.

"I didn't mean that." She lowered herself to the gazebo floor, and the clouds shifted around her, thickening like a cushion. Green eyes watched him with intensity that prickled along his skin, stinging. "You know who I am."

"Oh, ho," he inclined his head. "Subtle." The fae didn't ask for introductions, not addressing those they did not already know unless first addressed. "And what do I get, for telling you my name?"

Her shoulders lifted and fell gracefully. He'd seen more beautiful physiques, but in that moment she was the most precious creature in any world to him, simply because she could see. Overwhelmed, he popped to the other side of the gazebo. She wouldn't remember him regardless, and it didn't matter how she received Matera's message. He could have written it on a wall and left it at that.

But Rizen had wanted to be seen, if only for a moment. Apparently his lesson had yet to be learned.

"I'm sorry," Alexandra called, searching for him.

He tried to speak, but his throat had dried, which was ridiculous since he controlled this world. A droplet floated before him, and he sipped it to calm his pounding heart. *She won't remember,* he reminded himself. The message, yes, but not him. "Rizen," he croaked.

Her head twisted to find him. "Rizen," she repeated, and his legs could no longer support him.

He caught himself at the last moment, resettling to a seated position on the wall.

"Are you all right?"

The tenderness was too much. "Never you mind!" Startled, she leaned away from him, but he embraced the familiar resentment. "Learn to live in the mortal world, Alexandra," he spat out.

Her eyes widened. "Am I… I'll never return?"

"You cast a spell. We all have to live with consequences."

"Do you know what spell, Rizen?"

His fist pummeled the wall beneath him. He'd meant to end the dream. But she had used his name. "No."

Her gaze fell.

"But spells have loopholes," he found himself saying.

Her head snapped up, both eyes focusing on him.

He was still a fool. "Find the loophole." A soft smile. This had to end. "Goodbye, Alexandra."

He raised his hand to wipe the dream away before she could prolong it. Her parting thought echoed in his head. *Thank you, Rizen.*

Chapter 4

When Allie awoke, all she felt was scratchiness and a somewhat hard surface. She couldn't see the sky. She was walled in. A dim light shone over her, blocked by fabric behind her head.

Mortal realm.

Learn to live in the mortal world, Alexandra.

She shot up, searching for familiarity. The two doors sparked an indistinct memory. The writer had stiffly brought her here after their dinner. He hadn't walked in with her but had offered use of the bed. The second door was the bathing room. He'd promised to leave her something in there—something useful.

Allie threw off the covering and rose. She had slept in the clothing he had lent her. No wonder her skin still felt constrained and irritated. At least it would have some respite as she washed.

The bathing room also had two doors. Allie crouched down to examine one of the knobs, searching for a securing mechanism. A little button rested in the center, so Allie pushed it. It clicked and remained pressed in. She jiggled the knob, and the button popped back out before the door swung open in her hand. She palmed it closed and pressed the button again, then mimicked the motion on the other door. A thin stretch of fabric blocked the single small window, set high in the wall.

Finally she felt safe removing the binding mortal cloth. Unlike nymphs and some of the other muses, Allie wasn't comfortable with public nudity, but clouds felt nothing like the restrictive pieces she had been wearing since the previous night. Her whole body sighed with relief once she had peeled them off.

Now she could focus on the new room. A purple, folded cloth rested beside the washbasin, above which hung a mirror. The floor was smooth under her feet, with a hint of pale green. Two small, light-blue covers rested on the floor. Closed wooden cabinets lined the far wall and filled the space under the washbasin. Metal rods protruded from the walls near both doors. A larger basin rested in the corner beside her, blocked off with glass.

Allie tugged on a small metal knob, and half the glass door swung toward her. She peered inside then stepped over the side of the basin. A shiny cord with a round end hung from one wall. Taking it down did nothing, so she replaced it. Two golden knobs rested alongside a hooked spout pointing into the basin, with a flat stick pointing up in between.

She moved the stick first, pushing it gently. It shifted toward her, but nothing else happened. She pushed it back. Twisting one of the knobs was next. Chilled water sprayed her from above, and she quickly twisted the knob the opposite way. She pulled the glass closed and tried again.

The other knob brought hotter water. Twisting both at once allowed her to find a comfortable, soothing temperature. Sighing, Allie tried to enjoy the water coursing over her body. Her long hair clung to her skin, and she lifted it away, unused to the wet weight. The spray beat relentlessly against her skin. In fae lakes, water buoyed her hair as she relaxed. She avoided lingering in the waterfalls.

Allie dropped her hair over one shoulder. Another change to which she must become accustomed.

Maybe he should pull the curtain open. Not because Alexandra had suggested it. But what he was doing, what he'd been doing every morning, still wasn't working. Brett brushed his hand through his hair, tugging at the locks. Should he get a haircut?

Hadn't Einstein or someone postulated that writing things down right after waking up was supposed to provide the best ideas? Brett had been trying that for a while, but he'd written nothing but drivel. Nonsensical thoughts. Nothing was getting his next book going. He'd even taken to sleeping on the couch in his office, so he could stare at the screen until late into the night, and then stare some more whenever he woke up. On the plus side, that meant giving up his bed last night hadn't really been an issue.

The soft sound of water pouring turned his head, as if he could see through the walls separating his office from the master bathroom. Still, it was a safe bet Alexandra was taking a shower.

That actually did inspire him, bursts of images popping into his head. Alexandra leaning over to turn the shower on, holding her hair up so the water could hit her skin; droplets coursing down her breasts, and pausing in her belly button, or flowing lower. Not quite the type of scene he needed for his book.

Or was it? It'd definitely be an unexpected change for his readers.

Brett shoved his chair away from the desk. He needed a cold shower.

He wanted a steamy one.

How had he gone from wanting to get rid of the unexpected stranger in his house to wanting to keep her close? Intimately close. It wasn't like he didn't have a sex life, occasionally; he'd just always kept any woman he was with away from his home. After all, it'd been his grandparents' house. And because of Vicky. He wasn't stupid enough to have sex with strangers anyway, but the casual flings he'd had, he'd kept out of sight of his sister. Since they'd moved away from their parents, she'd only met one of his girlfriends. Good thing she was studying abroad this semester, because there was no way he could reasonably explain keeping this stranger, beguiling as she was, around. If Vicky ever did something this stupid, he would beat the guy up, or call the cops. Or both.

Brett stalked out of the office. The usually cheerful living room mocked him. The distant shower shut off.

Alexandra would be getting out, probably toweling herself dry.

He could take a shower in the spare bathroom, but he'd left his toothbrush and razor in the main one. And if she came out now and saw him, his need for a cold shower would be obvious. Especially since all he wore was boxers. *Damn it!*

He strode back into the darkened office. Without the light on, only a thin stream of sunlight illuminated his desk. He snatched his jeans from their spot on the floor and stuffed his legs into them, then sank onto the couch. What the hell was he doing?

Allie had attempted to squeeze all the excess water from her hair, but the heavy braid was soaking through her top regardless. Why hadn't it dried as soon as she had finished bathing? Mortal women had long hair, and she had never seen them with it sopping wet. Hers had also become a different color, darker. Hopefully it would return to normal after it dried. Assuming it did dry. Was there some particular trick she hadn't employed? The writer would think her an imbecile.

She didn't hear anything when she exited the bathroom. The door to Brett's workspace was slightly ajar. Allie paused outside it. How did humans announce their presence?

A sharp sound on the wood, that was what had always preceded someone interrupting one of her charges. She tapped her fingers against the door, producing a muffled sound. The door swung away from the light pressure. Allie dropped her arm.

"Good morning," Brett said from the darkness. Sunlight filtered in from the windows behind her, and Allie turned partially from the doorway so she didn't block the rays. Brett stood and walked toward her stiffly. His eyes fell to the damp spots on her top created by wisps that had escaped her unraveling braid. Allie swiftly crossed her arms over the offending areas.

Brett's eyes jumped to her face just before he brushed past her. She bumped the wall in an attempt to clear his path. He disappeared around the corner across from the bathroom then reappeared almost as quickly with a new garment, which he held out to her. This one opened in front and would fully cover her arms, as the very first one had. Allie took it and slipped her arms in, resettling her hair over the back. It was somewhat fuzzy on the inside. A type of fastening stretched down both edges of the opening, but Allie didn't see how it would come together. Trying would simply make her appear even more foolish, so she left it unfastened.

She still had to acknowledge the gesture. "Thank you."

"Sorry, I don't have a hairdryer."

A hair dryer. So perhaps he didn't think she was entirely ridiculous. Allie was working on crafting a platitude to respond when he stepped forward. He tugged the corners of this garment closed, connecting two metal pieces at the bottom with a click, then pulled a small piece up, which brought the fastening together.

A subtle warmth radiated from him, reaching her despite the remaining distance. The moment seemed to freeze. Suddenly, the beginnings of a beard covering his jaw fascinated her, drawing her gaze to the soft, pale curves of his lips.

Before she could remember to breathe, Brett stepped back. Allie blinked, and her lungs resumed working. What had just happened? It was as if her mind had ceased to function. Was this a part of becoming mortal? No wonder they needed muses!

Brett speaking drew her out of her contemplation. "I'm going to jump in the shower. Then we can go get some breakfast, okay? And talk."

He was watching her, though differently than the night before, his expression lacking the distrustful, wary intensity. Had he formulated a plan for ridding himself of the nuisance she now was? He continued to wait for a response.

"Of course," she forced out.

Brett nodded and turned away to enter the bathroom. Alexandra wandered out into his living room and toward the windows, which exposed a breathtaking view of the city. Apparently, his house stood atop a hill or mountain. More importantly, she had to cease behaving in ways unacceptable to mortals. Heracles' tasks seemed in that moment less daunting.

✧ ✧ ✧

Brett held the door of Dreams to Dishes open, waiting for Alexandra to step through. She had yet to say much of anything today, though she had peered curiously out the window on the brief drive over. She paused just inside the doorway, similarly peering about the small diner. Brett led her to his favorite booth then waited until she sat down.

Kristie hurried over soon after with two mugs and a coffee pot. She squinted at his companion, undoubtedly surprised to see anyone but Vicky with him.

"Thanks, Kristie."

She flashed him a smile. "Hey, Brett. Should I bring a menu?" A dismayed shout from another table drew her attention before he could answer. "Be right back," she said over her shoulder.

Brett nodded, not that she saw. She'd make her way back after cleaning up the spilled coffee. Alexandra was watching Kristie help the family involved in the spill. "What're you in the mood for?" he asked.

Her head snapped around to him. "I'm…not certain?"

Her words wouldn't have felt strange if not for the question in her tone. She was almost asking his permission to be unsure. "I can order for both of us."

She nodded jerkily.

Brett added sugar to his coffee before taking a large sip. Her mug stood untouched. "They have good coffee here."

She considered the mug in front of her, then slowly reached for it and brought it to her face. She sniffed it as though it were a foreign substance then tilted the edge into her mouth. He doubted she consumed more than a couple drops. Her brows drew together, slightly crinkling her skin.

"Not a fan?"

Kristie reappeared at his side then, and Alexandra set down the mug. Her shoulders dropped with obvious relief. Brett focused on ordering. Since she'd so clearly dreaded drinking the coffee, he added a glass of orange juice. Kristie rattled back the order, then stuck her pencil behind her ear, winked, and sidled off.

That got Alexandra's attention. "The two of you are friends?" she asked, watching the waitress walk away.

"I come here a lot."

She fingered the paper placemat, looking back to him.

"It, uh, it gets me out of the house, out of my head. I figure it's better than being a recluse." Sometimes, when he was on a roll, the diner's staff were his only contact with the outside world.

Her lips and brows curved quizzically. "You seem quite sociable."

Her bizarrely innocent confusion was almost endearing. "I can be. I don't always like to be, though." He sipped his coffee.

Allie glanced around the diner, her eyes pausing on every sign. Brett took in the deeply red wisps framing her pale face, with the three perfect curves of her mouth and her large, vibrant eyes. She brushed back a lock of hair that had come loose from her drying braid.

Brett followed the motion of her hand, around her ear and down, past her breasts, to the edge of the table. He forced himself to look away and take another sip. "I was thinking, we should probably get you some clothes after we eat."

Alexandra's only response was a sharp set of shallow nods, undermined by an uneven lift to her shoulders.

Kristie bounced over with their meals: eggs benedict with a generous helping of home fries for him; spinach-and-cheese omelet and a short stack of pancakes for her. Plus the orange juice. Alexandra sat statuesque with tension, watching the plates as though the food posed a threat. By her expression, you would have thought Kristie had brought them lumpy gruel not even fit for Mr. Bumble's workhouse, not the appetizing dishes now on the table.

"Hey." Her panicked gaze flew to his face. "This'll be way better than dinner last night," he coaxed.

She exhaled with a twitch of the lips but didn't move to touch her food.

Kristie swept by to refill his coffee. She started to move away but then noticed Alexandra's stony expression. "You all right, there?" She glanced at the untouched food and then to Brett for confirmation. "Do—do you want something else?"

Alexandra shook her head slightly then offered Kristie a strained smile. "It's wonderful. Thank you."

"Sure." Kristie hesitated about leaving, but another customer called for her. Brett finally noticed the smudged makeup around her eyes, the uneven tilt of her ponytail, and that her earrings didn't quite match. Before he could comment, she added, "Give me a shout if you need anything," and stepped away.

Alexandra reached for the juice. She smiled after tasting it. More relieved than he should have been, Brett picked up his utensils. She mirrored his movement. Brett exhaled and popped a cube of potato slathered in hollandaise into his mouth.

Chapter 5

She could do this. She had, mostly successfully, navigated breakfast out in the public mortal realm. It had actually been quite delicious, other than the "coffee." The yellow mixture—"omelet"—had been almost fluffy, mixed with a bit of flavorful ooze. The combination of "pancakes," the melting ball they had come with, and sticky sauce—"syrup"—which Brett had insisted she try had played with her taste buds. Other than the faltering start, she hadn't noticed any faux pas she may have committed.

Then again, eating was a different matter than "getting clothes." Purchasing clothes? Brett had somehow paid for their meal with a small card. Then they had returned to the car, to move through streets filled with concrete, occasional bricks, and artificial lights.

Now they had entered the "Super Store." Allie was still trying to determine if that meant the store itself was somehow exceptional, or if the "super" described its products. At the very least, the size of the hall in which they stood was quite impressive.

Fabrics in all manner of colors and fashions hung around them and on the walls, and more seemed to stretch in every direction, though other articles were evident in the distance.

Selecting attire could not possibly be as complicated as she was picturing. Allie clenched her jaw and tried to formulate an approach to the endless options.

A young black-haired girl stepped in front of them with a wide smile. "Can I help you?" she asked Allie.

Caught off-guard, Allie opened her mouth to decline, but Brett smoothly stepped in. "Hi,"—he read the tag on the girl's shirt—"Erika. My friend here is in from out of town, and the airline lost all of her luggage." Erika's smile dropped, and her eyes widened. "She's not used to our sizing system and all that, so maybe you could help her find something? She's stuck here with no clothes at all, and she's supposed to be here for at least a few weeks."

A few weeks?? Inconceivable.

"Oh sure!" Erika turned to Allie again. "Do you have an idea of what you'd need?"

"What do you think?" Brett interceded again. He clearly wasn't genuinely asking, but she was grateful for his continued assistance. "A pair of jeans, a skirt, some slacks, and a bunch of tops? Plus, you know"—he looked at Erika with a crooked half smile and raised eyebrows—"unmentionables?"

Erika's eyes scanned Allie's current outfit. She resisted the urge to cross her arms over her body as though she were still naked. If she hadn't known Brett made up stories for a living, she would have been in awe of his smoothly concocted tale. Then again, perhaps he had been contemplating how to account for her presence and obvious lack of common knowledge since they had left his home. Thankfully, he seemed inclined to come to her assistance.

"I think we can figure something out," Erika finally stated. Her lips moved into a more genuine smile. She gestured toward one of the aisles of hanging cloth. Allie clenched her fists and stepped in the suggested direction.

A whirlwind of selections later, a small room Erika had unlocked for Allie's use was filled with both piles and hanging articles of clothing. Brett had abandoned them when they had stepped into the section of the store above which hung a large sign with the label "lingerie." Erika had directed her toward boxes of what she called panties, guessing at a size. Allie had seen such flimsy pieces on women in photographs on the walls of her charges' homes, or in their minds as they described lascivious scenes. As it turned out, these were intended to be worn beneath other attire.

"Do you like thongs?" Erika asked, holding up a scrap of fabric with thin strings attached.

Allie hastily shook her head.

"What about bikinis? Or boy shorts? These are really cute!" She held two bright purple options with pink and yellow hearts. At least these consisted of more fabric, which would allow her some modesty—and some clues as to how they were to be worn. One looked more like the garments worn by men, so Allie chose the "bikinis," with two solid pieces of fabric, although also joined by thin strings.

Erika tossed some more colorful options of that style into the plastic bin she held. "So your friend is pretty cute. And it's sweet of him to help you with all this. Are you two together?"

"Not right now." What a silly question, since he was obviously not beside her.

"Oh, is it the distance? That can be so hard on a relationship. My last boyfriend and me, we broke up when he left for college." She steered Allie to a nearby section as she chatted. "What about bras? Do you know about what your measurements are?"

Allie shook her head apologetically. It made sense that garments came in a variety of sizes, as did the humans who wore them, but that made selecting them nearly impossible right now. Clouds easily molded to the form and the mood of the particular muse. Everything was more complicated here.

"Well, we can check. If you don't mind. I mean, no one's around."

She had no idea what Erika meant, but it wasn't as though she had many alternatives. "All right."

"Okay, so just unzip the hoodie, and hold up your arms." Allie obliged with a mixture of dread and curiosity. Erika plucked an item off one of the protruding pegs. She opened the fastening then reached around Alexandra, under the sweater. She brought the open edges together, overlapping them. "Way too big. A couple sizes down should do it, though. We'll have to guess with cup sizes, but you're probably a D or double. Do you see any styles you like?"

Before Allie could answer, more articles plopped into the bin. Erika led her back toward the private room. "Why don't you try these, and if they don't work we'll try something else." She thrust the bin into Allie's hands and pushed open the door with a smile.

Allie stepped into the overflowing room. Was she supposed to try each article on separately? In some combination with each other? A few hundred years ago, women's fashion had consisted of complicated layers, but surely that had changed by now.

"Try a pair of panties on over the ones you're wearing now, and then you can choose the others to match their size." Erika directed through the door.

Allie set the bin down and dug toward the bottom, where she found a simple black "bikini." She slipped off the rubber shoes Brett had loaned her and tugged the fabric over the bottoms. She looked ridiculous, but the fabric didn't press into her flesh much or fall off, which seemed about right.

"How's it going?" Brett asked from the other side of the door.

"Oh, pretty well. Lots of things to try, so it might be a while," Erika answered, giggling. Was the young girl laughing at her? Allie wouldn't fault her.

"Hey, Alexandra?" Brett called.

"Yes?"

"You can choose some things you'd like to wear right away. Right?"

"Oh, totally," Erika's voice confirmed.

"Just rip off the paper tags and hand them to Erika for the things you want to wear right now."

"All right." She had seen the paper labels on every item in the store. Apparently, they were not a part of the style. She slipped the "panties" down over her hips and detached the tag. A little piece of plastic poked out, but removing that would likely tear the fabric. Pressing her hand against the door to ensure it stayed shut, Allie slid off the bottoms she wore and put the panties on again. She set the tag on a small, unfilled shelf that protruded slightly from the wall. So far so good.

Less than five minutes later, she reconsidered. Contemporary "bras" seemed only slightly less torturous than ancient bustiers, and she was fairly certain mortal women had had help with those. She stood in the tiny room, contorting her body to see the fastening behind her back in the mirror as she attempted to latch the tiny hooks. Erika and Brett spoke amiably outside, though she couldn't quite make out what they were discussing. Asking for help would only further prove her incompetence, but she had already tried switching among the various options Erika had selected.

She couldn't stand there in nothing but the bottoms Brett had loaned her indefinitely. "Erika?" she called quietly. A giggle floated to her. She raised her voice slightly. "Erika?"

"Yeah? You all right in there?"

"Sorry to interrupt…"

"Oh, it's not a problem." Feet appeared on the other side of the door.

Allie dropped her voice to avoid Brett hearing her discuss "unmentionables." "I think, perhaps, the size isn't quite right for the… Well, I can't quite hook them." She squeezed her eyes closed, not that Erika could see her through the door.

"The bras?"

Oh, how she missed her invisibility. Maybe if she wished desperately enough, all of this would turn out to be no more than a nightmarish dream. Unfortunately, muses didn't dream. *Learn to live in this world…* The delivery of that message was proof enough that she was mortal. *Temporarily! Maybe.*

New bras appearing over the top edge of the door drew her back to the present. "Here," Erika called. "These hook in front. But you could also,"—she lowered her voice—"you can hook the others in front, then twist them around before putting on the straps. I'd never really thought about it, but I wouldn't have guessed bras are that different in other places. Where'd you say you were from?"

Allie shook her head at the influx of information. She settled for saying, "Thank you," and accepted the new bras. Some twisting, snapping, and unbecoming jiggling later, she found a moderately comfortable option that supported the mortal weight of her breasts in a similar way to the photo attached to the bra. She ripped the tag off and laid it atop the one from the panties, then surveyed the multitude of tops, skirts, and pants that still awaited her, not to mention the various other bras.

Seeking the least restrictive option, she selected a gray skirt in an airy material, with tiny tendrils of a floral pattern. It reached to slightly above her knees and swirled gently as she shifted her weight from one foot to the other. She slipped on a simple, white top, and tried to judge her reflection the way a human might. Was there insufficient color? Did the styles clash in some horrifyingly embarrassing way?

"How're you doing in there?" Brett asked softly.

"Oh! Sorry, I didn't intend for this to—"

"Don't worry about it. Take your time," he interrupted as though he'd read her mind. "I just wanted to make sure you'll have enough. There's a washing machine at the house, but you should still get enough for two or three weeks, so you don't have to keep doing laundry."

"All right." How much did humans wear in "two or three weeks"? Would she really be trapped here that long?

Foreseeing half her thoughts yet again, Brett added quietly, "You know, more uh, undergarments than other stuff. Probably a bunch of tops. Just get everything you like, don't limit yourself."

Allie surveyed the assortment around her.

"Okay?" he asked in her silence.

"If—if you say so." Her shoulders slumped of their own accord. She had to try everything?

It had taken a few hours, but they'd finally made it out, carrying bags bursting with new clothes. And lingerie. Brett had seen the many options the salesgirl had brought and kept imagining Alexandra slipping in and out of them. It was a good thing the clerk had been there to distract him somewhat. He'd also taken the time to gather some socks, a hairbrush with some hairbands, a jacket, and some toiletries for her. At least his time taking care of Vicky was serving him well, making this easier.

Alexandra hadn't blatantly taken advantage of his offer, selecting a sparse wardrobe for a woman, and even protesting at his insistence that she needed more than one skirt and pair of jeans, but his credit card had still ultimately gotten a workout. And they weren't done; she needed shoes. On the other hand, seeing her in her new outfit almost made up for it. A soft, forest-green top with fluttering sleeves crossed over her breasts, offsetting the brightness of her hair and the paleness of her skin. She'd matched it with a similarly soft skirt that flowed easily over her hips.

Moments like this reminded Brett that he knew way too much about women's clothing. On the plus side, that knowledge came in handy when he wrote about his female characters. Still, he hadn't spent this much time in clothing stores since Vicky's early teenage years, and he hadn't exactly wanted to relive the experience.

Maybe the shoe store would go more quickly. At least shoes were easier to size.

Fifteen pairs of shoes later, Alexandra had selected a pair of delicate sandals with a memory foam insole and a gray pair of ballet slippers or Mary Janes or something—flat ones, with a rounded fabric toe. He was mildly disappointed she hadn't tried on any of the heels, but those thoughts really had to stop.

As lovely as Alexandra looked in her new outfit, she also seemed completely worn out. The faint color she had previously had in her cheeks had faded. The corners of her mouth drooped slightly, and the nervous tension of earlier had been replaced with an eerie stillness. Most women would have been thrilled at the new wardrobe. Alexandra gazed listlessly out the car window.

Brett tapped his fingers on the steering wheel. Perversely, the silence he usually loved was killing him. Maybe because in the silence, his mind tried to figure out what in the world had possessed him to furnish a wardrobe for the woman who had, as far as he knew, broken into his home. As if she would be staying with him indefinitely! Which apparently she would be, because for whatever reason, he didn't want to turn her over to either set of authorities that would get her out of his life, and she didn't seem inclined to leave. He had to find something to think about other than the endless loops of chastisement and reasoning.

"So, do you have a nickname, or does everyone call you Alexandra?"

It took a couple seconds, but her head turned in his direction. "Most call me Alexandra."

"What about the ones who don't?" Who were they—her parents? A boyfriend? People wondering at her disappearance from their lives? She didn't answer, but she didn't resume looking out the window either. At a red light, he looked at her. "Alex? Lexie? Andie?" *What else?* "Xandra?"

She slightly shook her head. He'd hoped for at least a smile at his bizarre guesses.

"Allie," she finally volunteered.

Brett nodded. "Should I stick with Alexandra?"

"Whatever you prefer."

What had happened to the feisty, impassioned woman he'd first seen examining his office less than a day ago? All of the challenge and life within her seemed to be draining away.

Allie couldn't bring herself to chat or even be pleasant. She genuinely appreciated the writer's overwhelming generosity. Unfortunately, their day had also demonstrated precisely how dependent she was on Brett, on his benevolence, for however long she was to be in this realm. The many bags filled with items he had purchased taunted her, their presence proof she wouldn't regain her true form for an indeterminably long time, if ever.

She was trapped, stuck wearing binding mortal cloth and living walled off from nature. And what would happen when Brett was no longer willing to accept a stranger living in his home? She was at his mercy, and that unavoidable reliance was torturous. At least as a muse, her role had been clear. What was she expected to do in this world, other than searching for a way back? Not that she had any idea where to begin. The best clue at her disposal was the vague memory of her first and only dream. *Find the loophole.* But what was the spell the weaver had insisted she had cast? How could she have cast it without knowing? Moreover, how could she unravel its text if she didn't know what the original had been?

Brett unceremoniously placed the bags he held onto the bed in which she had slept, and Alexandra followed suit without thinking. Where would everything go? Presumably all of the furniture with storage compartments was already filled. She also couldn't expect him to continue sleeping in his workspace.

"I have an idea." The proclamation distracted her from the incessant whirl of her thoughts. Brett stood at the other edge of the large bed.

Allie couldn't bring herself to ask, so she raised her eyebrows in what was hopefully a curious gesture instead.

"C'mon," he said and headed out of the bedroom. Apparently he wasn't in a talkative mood, either.

Allie drew in a steadying breath and slowly exhaled. When that didn't help, she inhaled again and followed him. She didn't have much choice.

Chapter 6

Brett was waiting outside the door to the room for cars attached to his home. He opened the door, quite decorously, and Allie obediently stepped through. Where did he want to go now? Presumably, having expended so much effort on furnishing her with a selection of clothing and the like, he wouldn't take her into the middle of some wasteland and abandon her there, though she couldn't rule out that option with any amount of certainty.

A part of her wanted to remind him that he had yet to sit down and write today. Apparently ingrained habits hadn't disappeared with her transformation. She had particularly detested working with those who couldn't be bothered to invest their own time in their art. Granted, she could hardly fault Brett for being distracted by helping her. Rather than inspiring his writing, she was preventing him from working. Perfect.

Brett drove them without comment. His fingers tapped an erratic rhythm. They didn't seem to be in the car for particularly long, but the view around them began changing. Houses moved further apart and were interspersed with more vegetation and fewer artificial lights.

When he turned onto a winding road, the concrete disappeared almost entirely. Allie sat straighter in her seat. Trees popped up among grounded vegetation. She bit her lip. Perhaps she could ask him to stop for a little while?

Before she could decide, Brett pulled the car onto a small patch of cleared ground, covered with tiny pieces of stone. There were no other vehicles or humans in sight. That theory about him abandoning her might not have been too inaccurate. Then again, surrounded by the infusion of nature, Allie wasn't in that moment certain she would mind. When Brett opened his door, she eagerly copied the motion.

He led her around a small copse of trees beside a wooden cottage. Allie gasped as their path revealed a small lake, surrounded by colorful pinpoints of flowers and edged with more trees. The path they were on trailed down to grassy spots with wooden tables, then snaked around, disappearing within the trees.

Allie looked to her companion, wondering why he had stopped. A small smile tugged at the naturally upturned corners of his lips. Perhaps he had listened to her the night before? In that instant, it hardly mattered. Allie beamed in response then rushed down the path.

She couldn't see them, but nymphs certainly regularly frequented this place, gracing it with the delicate blooms that were a sign of their magic. Her lungs luxuriated in the invigorating air. Allie meandered to the edge of the trees, running her hands over the pleasant ridges of their bark.

When she turned back toward the still water, Brett was watching her. His brows had drawn together almost imperceptibly, and his smile had neutralized. Watching wasn't the right word. He was contemplating her.

Allie knelt by a small collection of flowers, inhaling their delicate fragrance. There had been a sign in the diner, she suddenly remembered. *Help wanted.* Perhaps it was assistance she would be able to provide, and they would recompense her financially. Then she would be able to return the funds Brett had expended today. She would become less of a burden, but also less useless, and possibly somewhat less dependent!

Furthermore, she had noticed artists with drawing pads, and writers scribbling ideas on napkins throughout the diner. Brett's own frequenting of the place lent credence to the possibility that artists regularly came there. That meant some of her colleagues may pass through, and then perhaps recognize her and send assistance. Or, she would survive long enough that the passing sprite would make her whereabouts known. She didn't have close friends among her kind, but surely she wouldn't be left stranded.

The ideas flowed in abundant succession through her mind. Was this how humans felt when she inspired them?

Reluctant yet reinvigorated, she rose from the ground and strode back toward Brett, trailing her fingers in the vegetation around her.

Brett couldn't even blink. Aside from her vibrant hair, Allie melted into her verdant surroundings. He was afraid he'd close his eyes and discover she'd disappeared. She clearly drew energy from the greenery. As she walked toward him, rejuvenated, he was struck with the pure vitality reflected in the slight pinkness of her cheeks and the confidence of her stride.

She'd smiled so brightly at him earlier... All the vibrating anxiety had evaporated into the crisp air. He'd loved coming here before, but now he'd never forget the vision of her moving toward him that left him breathless.

Brett shut his eyes and swallowed. When he finally reopened them, she stood before him.

"This place is beautiful," she murmured.

He swallowed again and moved to one of the picnic tables. He stepped onto the bench and sat on the table, lacing his fingers together. "It's pretty great."

Allie watched the undisturbed lake. "There was a sign saying 'help wanted' at the diner."

"That means they're looking for another waitress," he explained, distracted by a gentle wind caressing her hair.

She turned to face him. "I would like to repay you for everything you purchased."

"Don't worry about it."

"How can you afford such generosity since you… Most writers aren't lavishly compensated for their efforts, as far as I am aware."

Brett wondered at the change in direction but let it go, stifling his natural curiosity. She was arguing in favor of returning his money, not taking more, and she wasn't wrong about his income. "Have you worked as a waitress?"

"No." Her posture sagged no more than a few millimeters. She came closer then lowered onto the bench beside his knee. "Do you believe it would be extraordinarily difficult to learn?"

The unabashed questioning in her eyes distracted him. Brett tore his gaze away to look over the water. "No, not extraordinarily." He shouldn't mind her wanting to work. Hell, he didn't mind. But thinking about her having a steady job at the diner and what that meant for her continuing to stay at his house was unsettling. Clothing was portable, or even returnable. Getting a job implied a longevity to the arrangement he didn't want to contemplate too carefully. Then again, working at a diner wasn't exactly a career.

"I would genuinely prefer to recompense you for your hospitality," she repeated.

Every time she offered to repay him, his mind jumped to the absolute worst implication. He was beginning to feel like a letch, especially since she was obviously disconnected from the sensuality that oozed from her—or she would have taken a very different tack to their first encounter, not to mention to her wardrobe selection. He had to keep his distance.

That would probably be easier to do if she wasn't with him one hundred percent of the time, regardless of however long she'd be around. Brett pushed up from the table and stepped to the ground in an easy motion, then took a few more steps. "Guess we could go talk to Hal, see if he'd be up for it."

Alexandra stood as well but paused to survey their surroundings, obviously unwilling to leave. Finally, her eyes landed on him. A soft, genuine smile curved her lips. "Thank you, for bringing me here. As well as everything else you have done, of course."

Brett nodded, once, then gestured for her to precede him back up the trail to the car.

"She has no resume, or references, and no experience as a waitress? I mean, no offense." Hal tilted his head in false apology. "But c'mon, Brett."

"She has me as a reference," Brett pointed out. They stood by the diner's cash register, talking to the unconvinced owner of Dreams to Dishes. The name reflected Hal's faded artistic aspirations. A decade ago, he'd given up and settled for surrounding himself with others' creativity at his tables. Brett had no idea what kind of artist he'd been, or if he'd been any good. The man did run a fine diner, though. "She's just a girl, down on her luck, who needs help getting her life on track. A job would go a long way to doing that." Brett hadn't written a word today, but his yarn spinning was getting a workout. "Just give her a chance."

Hal pursed his thin lips. Alexandra stood beside them, unobtrusively observing the exchange. "There's paperwork to fill out, legalities. You said she doesn't even have ID."

Damn. He really hadn't thought this through, even if it hadn't been his idea. "Isn't there some kind of trial training period, or something?"

"Yeah, there is. Still requires paperwork." Hal regarded both of them with narrowed eyes. "I don't need any trouble, especially with the IRS."

"Please," Alexandra chimed in beside him. "Isn't there any way?"

Considering she didn't actually need the job in any immediate sort of sense, her determination was kind of odd. Maybe she was playing to her audience, not that that was a comforting thought. Brett didn't comment, letting her seemingly earnest plea play out.

Hal sighed. "Look, I'm up for giving you a shot." Apparently Brett wasn't the only one charmed by her. Alexandra's eyes widened hopefully. "But you guys've gotta figure out the paperwork side of things."

Brett looked around the diner, seeking inspiration. He could just leave it at that; she couldn't claim he hadn't tried, but he didn't like failing. It was part of what'd been so frustrating about his writer's block—the unyielding reminder of failure that was the blank page. "What if you did it in my name?"

Both pairs of eyes turned on him: one hopeful, the other confused. "The paychecks would have to go in your name, then," Hal explained.

"That's perfectly acceptable," Alexandra answered without hesitation. Hal's eyes narrowed even more, if that was possible. "I'm certain we wouldn't have any disputes with regards to finances."

Brett stayed silent. If she had no access to a bank account or identification, this might actually be the only option, other than Hal paying her under the table, which he wasn't about to suggest.

"If the tough situation you're in is him right there, you can tell me right now," Hal stated seriously, eyes trained on Alexandra.

Brett hadn't expected that, but admittedly the situation seemed strange. Still, he'd never been accused of abuse, even so indirectly. He grit his teeth and hoped Alexandra would straighten out the well-intentioned man.

Her gaze bounced between Brett and Hal. "I don't understand...?"

"If there's a problem, you tell me. If he's threatened you, or put you up to this—"

She jerked back with widened eyes as understanding dawned. "Not by any means! Brett has been nothing but courteous and helpful," she assured.

Brett let out the breath he'd been holding. She could've just as easily thrown him under the bus. It wouldn't have been the first time someone did to get what they wanted, though in this case he still had no idea what that was.

Hal's dark eyes considered his frequent customer. Brett gazed back calmly.

"All right," he finally agreed. "Be in at nine tomorrow. We'll do the papers, and Kristie can show you around before the lunch rush. This *is* just a trial period," he cautioned at Alexandra's triumphant smile.

<h1 style="text-align:center">Chapter 7</h1>

People walk in, you say hello, and they pick a table. You swing by with menus, and then offer them coffee." Kristie moved around the bar as she spoke, pointing everything out in rapid succession. "Blue top's regular, orange is decaf. People might ask for half-caf, which is half decaf and half regular. Got it?"

"How do you measure?" Allie asked before thinking.

The blonde waitress crooked her eyebrows. "It's approximate." Allie nodded, but Kristie continued her walking instructions before she could respond. "You pour the coffee, and ask if they want something else to drink or if they're ready to order. Do drinks first, then write down the order. Repeat it back to them, and take it to the kitchen. Do a pass between tables with more coffee while Lenny's cooking.

"Food's kept warm here." She gestured to a metal shelf. "Wait until the entire order's up, then serve. Ask if they want refills on drinks. You should get in the habit of remembering what everyone's having, but for now you should just make sure with the customer every time you refill. Keep passing between tables."

Among, Allie silently corrected. Of course, Kristie wasn't crafting a literary masterpiece.

"Don't hover over them, but make sure if their cups are empty, you offer refills, and ask how their food is a few times during the meal. "

Kristie swiveled around and pulled a small notepad out of her apron pocket. Allie had received a similar one when Brett had brought her in. He and Hal sat in a corner, filling out some paperwork. Brett had suggested she avoid skirts, so Allie wore the "jean" bottoms and a purple top the tag had called a tee shirt.

"I'll handle the checks for now, but you'll have to learn to do that, too. Just write legibly." Kristie dug into a pocket and held out a round piece of rope. "And you should put your hair up."

Allie accepted the rope and surreptitiously examined Kritie's hairstyle. Braiding her hair would take too long, and she had never had to secure a style before. Presumably that was the purpose of the round rope; Brett had purchased an entire pack of them for her. Kristie's light hair had been gathered at the back crest of her head, and it coiled down from that point. Allie's hair was significantly longer.

"Now would be good. And get your apron on," Kristie directed brusquely then brushed past her to greet the two men who had come in.

Allie swept her hair into a loose braid that she already knew wouldn't hold in this realm; grabbed the notepad, apron, and rope; and rushed after Kristie.

"Hey, fellas," Kristie greeted with a significantly more friendly tone. "Coffee?"

Both men smiled at Kristie and exchanged pleasantries with her. When she turned to retrieve the coffee pots, Allie saw her eyes roll. "Go get the menus," she directed pointedly.

Allie bit back a retort and walked over to the stack of slick cards printed with the diner's offerings. For whatever reason, Kristie didn't seem to like her, despite the fact that her presence was intended to ease the mortal's workload.

"Here you go," she murmured to the men, handing them the menus. They smiled at her, but Kristie stepped in, close to the table to pour their coffee. She didn't quite push Allie, but stepping out of the way still seemed like the appropriate way to respond. Kristie wasn't the first colleague who hadn't liked her without a discernible reason. She had never quite connected with the other muses and had never belonged to one of their many social subgroups. On the other hand, she had never been required to work directly with them.

Kristie also wasn't the first human to treat her less amicably than they did others. The girl at the store, Erika, had been significantly friendlier with Brett than with Allie, and even Brett was more sociable toward virtually anyone than her. Not that she had a right or reason to expect otherwise. There was simply something about her that was unlikable, even among mortals.

Kristie wrote down the two men's order and tore the sheet out of the pad, handing it to Allie. "Kitchen."

Allie forced a smile and took the slip. She needed this employment, both to repay Brett and for a modicum of autonomy. Being as unpleasant toward Kristie as the human was to her would almost certainly cause this trial period to end prematurely. On the way back out to the dining room, she repositioned her hair, twisting it around her fingers. Kristie was talking with Brett and Hal, smiling widely.

"Don't worry about Kristie," a young man sitting at the bar said. A sketchpad lay in front of him, open to a blank sheet. Allie stepped closer. "She's just mad she has to share her tips," he continued conspiratorially. "But she'll be grateful a couple days from now, when she doesn't have to run around like a chicken with its head cut off during rushes."

Allie was uncertain how to respond. She dropped her gaze to the dishes in front of him. His mug was empty. Her hair fell forward. Allie brushed it back, clasping it with one hand. "Can I get something for you?" she asked. She probably should have offered sooner. Physically serving others wasn't in her nature, but she had no other option now than to learn, and quickly.

He surveyed her casually. Allie dropped her hand, and his lips twitched. "I should probably switch to decaf."

She turned to the pair of pots Kristie had shown her.

"Orange top," he reminded from behind.

"The point of getting help was to get someone helpful. Someone who knows what they're doing?" Kristie told Hal. Brett had never seen her so frustrated; flustered, harried, rushed, but not annoyed.

He wanted to step in, but Hal defended, "She'll learn."

Their trio moved from the corner toward the door. The paperwork was set, and all of them had to get back to work, though Kristie didn't have much to do at the moment for the faint smattering of patrons.

"You couldn't have hired someone with experience?" She didn't even bother to keep her voice down.

Brett searched out Alexandra. Her lips pressed together, and her chin notched up before she spun around to replace the coffee pot she held.

"You didn't have any work experience either," Hal pointed out.

"Yeah, well, I had plenty of experience serving meals to a bunch of rowdy men. And I'd been to a restaurant before. Seriously, aren't you going to tell her to get her hair out of the way?"

Brett didn't wait for Hal's answer. He had to get going, but he didn't want to throw Alexandra to the wolves either. He nodded at the artist at the bar then focused on the flowing red hair before him. "Hey."

She spun to face him, sending her hair flying. Brett stepped away from the other patron and held out the folded sheet he'd grabbed from his office. She moved with him.

"Directions, to get you back to my place. If you think you'll get lost, though, just give me a call. The number's on there, too."

She nodded a few times in rapid succession. "Thank you."

"Do you have something to tie up your hair?"

She slipped her hand into the standard-issue apron and produced a hairband. "Kristie gave me…this."

At the blank look on her face, Brett took the band and looped it around his thumb, then twisted it once and looped it over again, and again, until the band sat a bit too snugly, pressing on his skin. Her eyes watched the motion attentively. "Loop it around your hair like that, it'll hold," he told her quietly and handed the hairband back.

Her fingers slipped against his as she retrieved it. Brett was about to say something else, though he hadn't decided what, but Kristie appeared behind the bar. "Have a great day, ladies." He caught Alexandra's gaze and added, "Call if anything." When her lips twitched into a parody of a smile, he made himself leave. He couldn't exactly spend the whole day at the diner.

✧ ✧ ✧

Back in front of the computer, Brett changed his mind. He would have been equally productive back at the diner. In other words, not at all. Maybe sunshine really was the answer to all of his problems.

With a sigh, Brett pulled open the curtain behind his computer. Light streamed in, but it highlighted the dinginess of his office rather than chasing away the shadows, or the cliché cobwebs in his mind.

This room had been much more welcoming when it'd been his bedroom. It had been his refuge, once. He hadn't changed much in it since then, except to switch out the old bed for a futon. He hadn't even updated the computer, keeping his grandparents' old desktop. From a writing perspective, it offered him everything he needed: a reasonable Internet connection, a functional word processor, and a reliable auto save. He'd created the perfect writing cave, in which he'd written all three of his *Revelations* novels. Perhaps it really was time for a change, or at least a fresh place to start.

Brett shut off the monitor and pulled a notebook from one of the desk drawers. He grabbed a fistful of pens from the cup on his desk to scribble on an open page until he found one that worked.

Determined, he made his way to the living room and plopped onto the couch in front of the latticed bay windows. He knew the view was remarkable, and he didn't spend enough time enjoying it, but it faded before his eyes. All he saw was Alexandra, weaving through the woods, fingertips trailing through flowers that reached to her as though ready to whisper all their secrets. Not exactly right for a mystery novel.

Brett looked down at the lined page on his lap. Even his scribbles looked like a vague picture of Allie blending into the leaves around her. *Alexandra.* He shouldn't allow himself the false intimacy of using her nickname, even in his mind. Tapping his pen against the notebook, he looked out over the cityscape. This row of houses had been planned to showcase the view: innocent sweep of houses during the day; enticing, twinkling lights at night. But… Brett turned to a fresh page.

Even innocence could hide darkness.

Allie trudged back to Brett's house after Hal informed her that her shift was over. Cool air washed a refreshing silence over her. Thankfully, it was still light enough to read the directions Brett had written. Hopefully they weren't all that he had penned today.

Her feet were aching. Pain radiated from the abused soles up her legs. Standing for extended periods of time was not a new experience for her, but it had been significantly easier when her body was unaffected by the gravity of the mortal realm. If Brett was working, perhaps she could spend some time resting. At this point, even the relative comfort of his bed or couch would be a blissful relief.

She turned up the walkway to his home and paused despite the pervasive fatigue. She could see into his workspace, which meant he had pulled the heavy covering out of the way. Perhaps she could in fact be of some use for his writing, despite her current predicament.

Smiling softly, she continued to the front door Brett had promised to leave unlocked. It opened easily for her, revealing her progressively less infuriating charge sprawled before the windowed wall, surrounded by discarded scraps of paper.

"Hey," he greeted without looking up. Allie shut the door quietly but remained in the entryway for fear of disturbing his thoughts. Brett ceased writing and tossed down his pen. A smile spread through his features when he saw her but quickly disappeared. "How was your day?"

Her feet chose that moment to remind her of their displeasure. Allie continued into the house, stopping outside the wake of his writing efforts. "Demanding," she admitted. Customers had seemed to flood the diner after Brett's departure, and Allie's novice attempts to fulfill her duties had quite evidently frustrated Kristie rather than helped. "How was yours? Appears productive."

Brett stood from the couch and surveyed the results of his writing, brushing his hand through his hair. Allie shifted her weight to one foot in a futile attempt to relieve her discomfort. "It was fine," he commented dismissively. His eyes refocused on her. "You don't want to sit down? Your feet must be killing you." He paused. "Unless you're used to it?"

Sitting down sounded lovely. "Today was certainly outside my realm of experience."

Brett crooked his eyebrows.

Allie pulled the hem of her tee shirt away from her skin and shifted her weight to the other foot. Removing her binding clothing and refreshing her skin and muscles was particularly enticing. The only potential reason she could devise for relieving her body of its vestments was bathing. How had he called it? Shower. She had a feeling she would be utilizing the shower frequently during her stay. "Would you mind if I were to shower?"

Brett stilled with his gaze forcefully focused on her, reminding Allie of the novelty of her situation. He truly saw her. Apparently, he didn't want to, though, as he soon turned away and picked up his notebook. "By all means."

His dismissal stung, but her feet were finished being ignored, and Allie chose to focus on something she could actually affect.

After they had returned from the park the night before, Brett had insisted she continue to use his bedroom. He had removed some of his clothing to his workspace and even emptied a storage compartment for her use, in which she had placed the undergarments he had purchased. He had placed the miscellaneous items he had selected on his own—she had been relieved to discover these included a disentangling tool for her hair, which misbehaved atrociously in this realm—into the adjoining bathing room. Thankfully, the packaging for almost every piece included instructions for its use, as though the items were foreign even to the humans.

Allie closed the door and slipped off her shoes, then quickly removed the jeans and top. Instantly her body felt more at ease. Perhaps nudity had its benefits. Still, she darted into the bathing room to snatch the purple drying cloth. She discarded her undergarments and wrapped the cloth around herself, before finally allowing her feet a respite by lowering to the bed.

When it grew dark enough outside that he needed to turn on the lights, Brett finally paused from scribbling in his notebook. He had gotten some work done, but Alexandra kept popping into the scenes despite being wholly out of place, and he had no clue where he was going with these snippets. He'd been so focused, he hadn't even heard the shower, which was probably for the best. Alexandra in the shower definitely didn't belong in his writing.

Brett picked up the sprinkling of crumpled sheets and switched on the stylized modern sconces in the living room. The house was silent around him. Alexandra could be intentionally allowing him to work, or for all he knew, she could be doing something nefarious. Or she might have disappeared as noiselessly as she had first appeared. Strangely, he hoped not, even though that would have erased the unnecessary complications in his life that had arrived along with her.

He knocked on the door to his own bedroom. The light was off, and she didn't answer. He couldn't have imagined the whole thing, could he? It wasn't like he could have picked up a condition that caused hallucinations while doing research at Lyssa Iasso. Hopefully not, anyway.

Brett shook his head and knocked again, a little more loudly. If he had hallucinated everything, there was no reason he couldn't go in the room. The door creaked quietly as he opened it. Light from the hallway slanted into the room, crossing over Alexandra's feet. Brett stepped inside, temporarily blocking the light. Closer to the bed, he could see her chest moving with her breath. And that only a towel covered her, revealing the upper slopes of her breasts and a tantalizing peek at her hip.

He backed away, leaving her asleep, and shut the door.

He ate a dinner of leftovers at the kitchen island, unexpectedly lonely in the customary silence.

Chapter 8

Brett threw his arm over his eyes to block out the sunshine. Why had he ever opened that damned curtain? He didn't remember what time he'd finally crashed last night. He'd kept trying to write, but Allie continued to intrude in the novel's world. Alexandra…

He swung his body up and off the couch and padded out into the hall. She sat curled in one of the armchairs, washed in sunlight that caressed her garnet hair, with a book resting on her lap. She looked better than a dream. When she glanced up at him, the cacophony of his thoughts stilled as though he'd found the eye of their storm.

She jumped out of the chair, shutting the book. "Sorry! I… Is this all right? I didn't intend to disturb your things." She slid the book onto the oval side table beside her.

"It's fine." Silence. "Really, help yourself." His mind hadn't kicked into gear. "D'you want some coffee?" He headed toward the kitchen without waiting for an answer. Coffee would help.

Alexandra trailed him in. "No, thank you."

Brett busied himself with the beans, but the silence was annoying. "Do you have a shift today?"

"At ten o'clock."

He had no idea what time it was. He switched the coffee maker on and turned around. "Have you eaten?" She shook her head, and Brett turned to his fridge. There wasn't much inside. "I could whip up some eggs, if you'd like. Or French toast?"

"Either would be lovely, if you're certain it wouldn't be a problem."

"Sure, just, uh." The coffee was dripping steadily into the pot. Alexandra looked so fresh with the sunlight glancing off her pale skin. He must look like a disaster in comparison. And he hated eating anything before brushing his teeth. "I'll be right back."

When she heard Brett stepping back down the hallway, Allie poured him a cup of coffee. After repeating the motion count-less times the day before, it was already nearly automatic. He accepted the mug with murmured thanks and sipped the bitter drink enthusiastically. Allie opted for some water.

Brett set about extracting ingredients for their morning meal.

"Could I be of any assistance?"

He barely glanced at her over his shoulder. "I got it, don't worry." He downed the remainder of his coffee and refilled the mug.

Allie brushed a hand through her hair. "Well then if you don't mind, I suppose I should get prepared for work." Brett nodded. He seemed even less inclined to speak with her today. Practically the first thing he had said to her had been asking if she would be going to the diner. Apparently she had quickly worn out her limited welcome.

Allie strode to the bathing room, leaving the writer to his ministrations. Inside, she surveyed the items with pictures of hairstyles on them. She already knew the stretchable bands were useful, so she tucked a few into her pocket. Perhaps she should offer one to Kristie in return for the day before? Though she wouldn't expect the gesture to be appreciated by the antagonistic human.

A hard, rounded shape rested beside the bands, with the words "octopus clip" on the attached paper. On the picture, all of the woman's hair was gathered into a knot and held by the device. Allie disentangled its tentacles from the thick paper and set it aside, then attempted to gather her hair. When she finally twisted it into a coiled rope, she confined it with one hand and strove to secure the contraption. Everything fell to her neck.

Allie stared at her reflection then dug the "clip" out of her hair. Either her waist-long hair overwhelmed it, or she had missed some obvious piece of the process. No wonder Brett couldn't look at her after seeing her around the pretty women who could easily handle the basics of mortal life. She shook out the lingering coil to start again.

After a few more tries, Allie gave up on collecting all of her hair. Instead, she braided the locks that fell over her ears and pulled them back, securing them with the device. She shook her head softly to verify its hold. It would have to do.

Back in the kitchen, Brett had laid out dishes and jams, which she now recognized from her time at the diner. He stood by the stove, flipping pieces of French toast onto an already filled plate. Everything looked welcoming and smelled delectable. As a host, he was beyond reproach.

Despite some lingering pain in her feet and soreness she hadn't previously noticed in her arms, Allie enjoyed the walk to the diner. She took her time, knowing that frustrated glances from Kristie and endless customer demands awaited her. This position shed new light on the relative peace of being a muse. On the other hand, the few expressions of gratitude she heard from customers had been pleasantly surprising. Still, her impact on these people's lives could not compare to that which her presence had on the inventive creation of her charges. Though they never knew the role she and her colleagues played, each muse's personal touch could be felt on the lasting projects.

Unfortunately, Allie still had no ideas for how to return to her true state. The weaver's message had implied it was possible, despite her inability to find a starting point. It was unlikely she would have time to formulate a plan while at work. Yesterday's artist greeted her from his seat at the bar as she entered the diner. Allie refilled his coffee and headed to the back room to fetch her apron.

After Alexandra left, Brett shot off an email to Vicky then busied himself with typing up yesterday's notes. He edited as he went along, noting scenes he'd have to add and fleshing out some of the others, though none of it really seemed promising.

Needing to escape the expectant blink of the cursor, he minimized the window then opened up the FBI website. On the plus side, Alexandra didn't seem to be wanted for any crimes. Her photo also wasn't among the missing persons listings. Who was she that no one missed her?

A call from his agent interrupted the fruitless research.

"Hey, Sean."

"Hey, how's it going, buddy?" Sean tended toward overly friendly chatter, but his easy amiability suited Brett, usually.

"Eh, you know." Brett switched back to his notes. "Making a bit of headway on some new stuff."

"That's great! I can't wait to see what you've got in store for this next book. How about a preview?"

"To be honest, I've been pretty blocked until lately. There isn't much to show." Brett glanced with dread at his current word count, which mostly consisted of drivel he'd eventually cut, if it ever translated to an entire story at all.

"Well, hey, if anyone can pull this out, it's you. And progress is great. We just really don't want to lose momentum. I need at least a chapter and a solid synopsis before I can send out some feelers, and you know your readers are anxious to see more."

"I know." Brett passed his free hand over his forehead, using his thumb and middle finger to massage his temples. Sean needed material if he was going to make a sale, but the fact was, he had other clients, which meant other means of income. Brett had only his work for both himself and Vicky. And since he hated writing outlines or synopses before finishing a draft, he had lots of work ahead of him. "I'm working on it, Sean," he told his longtime agent sincerely.

"Well, hey, that's great that you've gotten past the writer's block. We should definitely chat when you have a solid feel for your story. I'm dying to know what you'll create next."

Yeah, Brett was, too. "Will do."

After discussing his recent sales and throwing around some promo ideas for his published books, they ended the call. Brett stared at the words on his screen, saved the file, and opened a new one. Maybe writing the scene of Alexandra with the flowers would allow him to move past it.

✧ ✧ ✧

A couple hours later, an uncharacteristically innocent story laced with magical elements claimed several virtual pages. Writing about Alexandra had driven him to an almost fairytale tone, so unlike his habitual mysteries. Talking flowers. He'd lost his mind.

Brett closed the file and glanced at the time. It was a little late in the afternoon for lunch, but he'd been too distracted to eat. He hadn't picked up groceries yet, either, which limited his options. He grabbed his keys and headed to the diner, a decision that had nothing to do with his enchanting, accidental houseguest.

Lunch stragglers still filled Dreams to Dishes, but his favorite booth was free. Kristie appeared with coffee almost as soon as he sat down on the worn red vinyl.

"Hey, there." She flashed him her customarily bright smile.

"Hey, Kristie. How's it going?"

"Oh, you know." She set down the coffee pot and pulled out her order pad.

"How's Alexandra getting on?"

Kristie dropped her hands to both hips, losing the smile. "Should I get her for you?"

"I'm good." He knew she hadn't been thrilled with having to train someone with no experience, but Alexandra couldn't be *that* terrible a waitress.

Kristie forced a blank smile he'd seen her give troublesome customers. "What can I get you?"

As soon as Brett had ordered, she rushed off. Brett drummed his fingers on the table and glanced around. He didn't recognize anyone in the diner, except the artist who almost seemed to live there, and didn't see any red hair. Not that he was looking. He was just there to get some lunch before heading to the store. Grocery shopping while hungry was a notoriously bad idea.

<h1 style="text-align:center">Chapter 9</h1>

llie spied an empty mug as she headed to the kitchen with a new order. "Would you like a re—" Brett looked up at her. "Fill," she finished.

His lips pulled up on one side. "Hey."

"Hello." She hadn't expected to see him. Somehow, having him there underscored how far out of her element she was. Waiting on tables was not why she had been sent here. It did provide her with something to say. "More coffee?"

Brett considered the empty mug. "You know, maybe I'll just have an iced tea. If you don't mind."

"Of course."

She would have moved away, but Brett asked, "So how're you getting along?"

She was the one supposed to be concerning herself with *his* work. Each time she had mentioned it, though, he had closed off. "Oh, well, it's calmed down a bit now. You arrived at a good time." He nodded, keeping his eyes on her. "Are you taking a break from writing?" she inquired with feigned nonchalance.

"Yep." He was watching her strangely, almost like when she had first materialized. Allie felt a peculiar compulsion to verify that her hair was in place, though thankfully the coffee pot and order pad she held prevented that. Brett blinked and subtly shook his head. "I'm gonna stop by the store when I leave, buy some groceries. I can swing by afterward and give you a ride if you'd like."

On the one hand, Allie didn't want to inconvenience him any more than her mere presence already did. On the other, the pervasive pain pounding through her feet begged her to accept the offer. It also reminded her she had work to do. "If you're certain it wouldn't be a problem."

"Not at all."

"Thank you." She could feel the muscles in her throat swallow. "I'll go bring you that iced tea," she finally stated, moving toward the kitchen without waiting for a response. If other empty coffee mugs awaited her attention on the way, she failed to notice.

"Won't even last a week," Kristie was saying as Allie entered the kitchen.

The comment brought her up short. Could she truly be trapped in mortal form for more than seven full days? It seemed an impossibly long time, and yet this was already her fourth day here. That realization made it more than likely, in which case she would strive to prove Kristie wrong, despite not understanding the source of the waitress' hostility. "Table fifteen asked for an iced tea." The diner's few tables were numbered fairly logically, which had made their order easy enough to memorize and allowed for a simple split among the staff. The numbers were also etched into the corner of each table, in case someone needed to verify. It was a clever trick.

Kristie straightened from the counter on which she leaned. "I'm off, so he's uh, all yours. Well, they all are."

Allie hadn't yet learned how to process customers' payments. If Kristie was leaving, the remainder of her shift would be disastrous. "What about—"

Kristie shrugged. "Figure it out. It's not exactly rocket science."

"Knock it off, Kristie," the chef, Lenny, chastised.

Allie gave him the order she still held and busied herself with pouring Brett's drink to avoid voicing her irritation. Writing and serving she could manage easily enough, but handling payments meant using mortal technology. She forced a steady stream of breath through her lungs. Perhaps Hal would demonstrate, at least once?

"I know, I know, I'm late." Another blonde woman, with slightly darker and more frazzled hair than Kristie's, backed into the kitchen while securing her apron. "You must be the new girl. I'm Wanda." Her eyes dipped to the tea in Allie's hand.

"I'll be right back," Allie stammered and left the kitchen. If Wanda was another waitress, at least she wouldn't be wholly on her own, even if that also meant there was another mortal whose hostility she would likely have to endure.

Allie placed the iced tea on Brett's table and kept moving without comment. She checked on customers at two more tables, all of whom were enjoying their food, and headed back toward the kitchen.

Wanda flashed her a smile as she exited with filled plates. "Hey, hang on a sec?"

Allie stepped out of the way, then around the bar. Wanda moved through the diner with an ease similar to Kristie's but somehow more fluid. She served Brett and twisted to find Allie, then joined her behind the bar.

"I didn't catch your name," she commented, reaching below the bar to pull out fresh rolls of silverware.

"Alexandra."

"It's only your second day, right? I missed you yesterday, 'cause Kristie had a longer shift. But I think we'll have crossing shifts from now on." She refilled the ever-present artist's cup without pausing. "So if you have any questions, just let me know. The important thing is to be as nice as possible, and people will forgive you just about anything. Well, so long as you don't spill anything on 'em. Right, sugar?" She winked at the artist.

He raised his coffee cup in reply. "You bet."

Allie couldn't help but admire the effortless amiability, a trait she herself so obviously lacked. Lamenting that wouldn't help her, but perhaps Wanda would. "Thus far, Kristie has been handling all of the checks."

"Oh, well no worries. Just grab me when someone wants to pay, and I'll walk you through it." A customer called, and Wanda assured, "You'll be fine," before stepping quickly to the table. Apparently she herself followed the advice she had offered Allie about being nice.

Allie surveyed the diner's occupants then went to check on her order, relieved. Even if the congeniality wasn't sincere, perhaps Wanda's approach would mean more pleasant interactions overall.

Brett swung back by the diner after picking up groceries and checked the time. Four forty-five. Alexandra still had fifteen minutes in her shift. He parked the car and headed inside. The artist was gone from his customary perch, and with only one table occupied, the diner felt a bit deserted. Or it would have, if it wasn't for the pleasant undertones of Wanda's chatter. Even Alexandra was smiling and looked more relaxed.

Wanda noticed him first. "Back again?"

"Just couldn't stay away." His gaze flicked to Alexandra, whose smile had dropped.

Wanda's keen eyes didn't miss the motion. "Oh. Well, you can knock off early, hon," she told Alexandra.

"Are you certain?" Her work ethic was almost admirable.

"Oh, yeah. I can handle this craziness. Wouldn't want to keep the writer waiting, or he might exact a nasty revenge in his books," Wanda teased in his direction.

"I'll return in a moment, then," Alexandra murmured. She skirted the bar with a smooth motion, as though gliding over the floor rather than stepping.

"What are you doing?" Wanda's voiced snapped him out of the bizarre contemplation.

"What do you mean?" Brett hooked a bar stool with his toes and sat down. "And I didn't know you read my books."

"That girl is sweet, but she's obviously not from this world."

Did she think Alexandra was supernatural? Many people had fae blood, according to the Celts. Did Wanda believe that?

"She doesn't belong slinging plates."

The diner. Of course she meant the diner. He'd dragged his story into the real world with him; it wasn't the first time.

"Hal said you're the reason she got the job," Wanda finished.

Brett's shoulders hunched. He was a private person in the best of circumstances, and he still wasn't really sure what had brought Alexandra into his life, or what had compelled him to have her stay. "Just helping her out."

Wanda's eyebrow crooked. "What's in it for you?"

"What do you mean, what's in it for me? I can't just help out?" He shouldn't be that offended by the implication; Wanda hadn't had the best luck with men. But it was the second time in three days!

"Most people wouldn't. Not without something to gain."

"I'm not most people." He wasn't expecting anything from Alexandra, was he? He hadn't been the one to suggest she get a job; she'd been the one who wanted to pay him back. For whatever reason, he hadn't even pushed her about how she'd appeared in the first place or who she really was. He also hadn't known Wanda thought so poorly of him. Her pursed lips and narrowed eyes said otherwise.

Finally she sighed and dropped the hand that had been on her hip. "I know. You're one of the good ones. But that girl? She's doesn't even know the game exists. And you could beat the best of 'em if you wanted to."

She wasn't wrong. Between the understanding of people that was required of writers and growing up with con artist parents, he couldn't deny that he read people pretty well. It was probably part of the reason that Alexandra's indiscernibility both fascinated and irked him. He didn't want to talk about it. "How's Jared doing?"

Like any proud mom, Wanda beamed at her son's name. "He's good. Finishing up eighth grade this year. Don't know what I'll do with that boy when he's in high school."

Brett smiled, thinking of her protective lecture of moments ago. "I'm sure you'll know exactly what to do. Jared's a good kid." Once in a while, Brett shot hoops with him. The kid was pretty sharp.

"Damn straight." Alexandra appeared at his side, and Wanda waved them off. "You two enjoy your evening." The pleasant words were undermined by the pointed look she shot Brett's way.

"See you tomorrow," Alexandra answered.

Brett just nodded before following her out.

Alexandra didn't say anything as they crossed the small parking lot. Had Wanda been right? Was the mysterious redhead really so innocently oblivious? He'd thought that may be a ploy, but Wanda generally had a good sense of people, when she wasn't trying to date them. And she erred on the side of caution, so if she thought Alexandra truly was the doe-eyed fish out of water… She not only had no defenses, she wouldn't even know she needed them.

"How're you and Kristie getting along?" he asked, sliding into his car.

"She is quite an efficient instructor." Her words held no trace of bitterness or sarcasm.

"So she's been helping you out?"

"I have learned quite a lot from her."

Brett glanced at her from the corner of his eye. She was looking dispassionately out the window. Either he'd read Kristie's displeasure incorrectly, or Alexandra wasn't one to complain. At least not to him.

Despite her living at his house, he really knew nothing about her. Technically, he'd now spent less time with her than her coworkers. "So did Hal give you a schedule?"

"For the next several days. He mentioned he would decide afterward whether to continue employing me."

Brett's fingers tapped impatiently on the steering wheel. Other than that one crack, she'd been so polite, careful of him. It bugged him. "Why do you want to work as a waitress?" he blurted out.

Her head turned toward him. "I told you, I would like to repay you for your expenses."

Oh. Right. Not that he knew why he'd gone through the trouble of buying her a wardrobe, or why he continued to let her stay. Part of him kept thinking of Vicky, further spurring his unexplained need to help and take care of Alexandra. If Vicky ever found herself in this kind of situation… Not that she would. She had him. Alexandra, at least so far, seemed to have no one, or no one she wanted around. Helping her out wasn't hurting him, other than the continued distraction of having her near, but his inappropriate imaginings were not a reason to throw her out in the figurative cold.

Brett pulled into the garage and killed the engine on autopilot. Alexandra waited by the car as he opened his trunk but didn't say anything. Her shoulders curled forward slightly, and her eyes trailed his every movement. When Brett started taking bags with groceries out of the trunk, she bit her lip from the inside, distorting the usually perfect line.

"I can get it," Brett assured. Her eyes dropped to the ground. "It'd help if you could get the door." Her chin danced up and down briefly, and she moved to the door, pushing it open. Brett elbowed the trunk shut and brushed past her, pausing for the briefest moment at the pleasantly sweet smell that clung to her from the diner, like she'd been dipped in freshly made French toast and syrup, with a side of bacon.

Allie would have been willing to assist Brett with sorting his purchase, but she had no knowledge of his system, so she would likely only disrupt his process, which left her standing somewhat awkwardly beside the standalone counter in the kitchen onto which Brett had lifted all of the bags.

He moved efficiently, emptying each bag in succession and hiding the items in the refrigerator—which she had learned at the diner kept mortal food fresh and nicely chilled—and a storage cabinet on the perpendicular wall. Her feet continued to ache, though less than the night before, as though their new pain sensors had been destroyed by the continued pressure. Nevertheless, sitting would have been welcome.

"Are you hungry?" Brett asked, balling all of the newly void bags into one mass. "I was thinking I'd get some more work done before dinner, but I can whip something together now if you'd like."

Distract him from his work? Absolutely not. "No, I would be fine waiting. Your work is important."

"Not saving any lives."

"Yes, you are," Allie protested without thinking. He spun calmly to face her, with two raised eyebrows. A whole host of emotions could be expressed with varying positions of the eyebrows. She had never noticed that before. The meaning of the arches above Brett's eyes was crystal-clear skepticism. "Reading brings distraction and comfort to many. It allows for a profound form of escape even without a physical parallel. For those in desperate situations, books can save lives, by providing hope, companionship, or simply an outlet. Of all forms of creativity, literature is the most transformative for and embracing of its audience."

The arches dropped and drew together, flattening into an almost uninterrupted line. Brett leaned against the counter behind him and crossed his arms over his chest. "Dancers, artists—they'd disagree with you."

"Dance, drawing, painting, sculpture, all allow brief glimpses into the world as their creator sees it. The creator travels an immense journey as he or she brings the project to life, but the audience is a guest on that journey, an observer of the result.

With writing, the author creates the path and then guides the reader through an entire voyage, which is undoubtedly different than the author's, but nevertheless more welcoming of its audience.

"Art can save lives by encouraging new creators, but literature can come to the aid of even those incapable of pursuing that form of creativity. Music would likely come the closest to a similar effect."

"You seem awfully certain."

Allie stiffened. She had said far more than had been prudent. "It's merely an opinion." *Based on hundreds of years of observation.*

Brett watched her for a prolonged moment then straightened. "I should get to work."

"Of course." She paused. "Would you mind if I borrowed a book?"

His head shook, displacing his gaze from her face momentarily. "I told you, help yourself." He headed toward the opening that led to the remainder of his home, then stopped, glancing back over his shoulder. "Should I wake you if you fall asleep?"

When the sky held only fading touches of the sun's colorful descent, Brett's steps sounded outside the room Allie had been occupying. Soon after, Allie heard noises emanating from the kitchen. She placed the mystery she had been reading—one of Brett's, since she had no other means of familiarizing herself with his work, as was her duty—then slipped out of the room and into his workroom.

She had followed the weaver's directions. Her position in this world felt relatively secure: Brett had easily if not enthusiastically integrated her into his world, and her employment provided a foundation for continued survival if that were to change. It was time to focus on discerning the reason behind her transformation and, more importantly, discovering the key to its reversal. A loophole.

As everything had happened in Brett's workspace, that seemed the most promising place to begin, so Allie stood in the middle of the small room, instinctively careful not to displace anything. Even in their natural form, muses could affect the objects around them. Not touching anything surrounding their charges was a deeply ingrained imperative, though occasionally mistakes were made. Fortunately, with winds, earthquakes, gravity, and other explanations humans created to avoid considering what they believed to be unnatural reasons, such instances were easily remedied, due in part to their rarity. An additional burst of inspiration could certainly help, distracting the charge in question.

Very little had changed in this room since her arrival. The couch apparently folded down into a wider surface, which was hopefully comfortable, since she had unintentionally rid Brett of his customary bed. The desk now held a notebook, and the machine beside it wasn't glowing. Otherwise, everything appeared the same as when she had arrived, expecting simply another uneventful assignment. When could she have cast a spell, as the weaver had claimed?

She surveyed the walls that, hopefully, encompassed the secret she sought and slipped her fingers below the straps of her bra, massaging the skin. The perpetual pressure of mortal clothing was gradually becoming easier to bear, but she longed to return to the weightlessness of her customary garb, and form.

The sole aberration she could discern from her usual assignments seemed to be the words that had flowed from her, through Brett's fingers. Words conceived in frustration, and so rapidly forgotten. Words that may very well hold the key to her transformation, and to the crucial loophole. If only she could access them through his machine. That would require knowing, at the very least, how to make it function.

The keys that lay on the table in front of the dark square held a mix of letters, numbers, and other symbols, none of which provided a clue for making the machine light up as it had before. She peered without moving at the rest of the machine, seeking out other buttons.

"What're you doing?" Brett's voice snapped her around to the doorway.

Allie reminded herself to breathe. She had done nothing that could upset him. She had certainly spent an abundance of time in writers' workspaces before, and she would again. *Hopefully.* "Attempting to ascertain something."

Brett's gaze rounded the space behind her. "You mean, how you came to be here?"

Well, that she actually knew, though he wouldn't welcome or credit the answer. Partial truths were her only recourse, even if she would have preferred otherwise. "I don't know what happened."

He held her gaze, at once reminding her of her entrapment here and enticing her to confide in this mortal who was her primary link to both her realm and this one.

"Dinner's ready," he finally said, stepping back, out of the doorway. He waited silently for her to leave his workspace then shut the door.

❖ ❖ ❖

Dinner had turned out pretty well, if he did say so himself. He'd baked some salmon fillets and an assortment of vegetables with some lemon slices and butter. Little noises of appreciation escaped Alexandra's throat after her first few bites, so apparently Brett's biased opinion wasn't too far off.

He didn't know what to make of finding her in his office. She hadn't been touching anything, and it wasn't like there was anything valuable in there, other than his notes, and his computer files. But the computer hadn't even been on.

It was suspicious, but Wanda's assessment felt right. Alexandra had definitely seemed out of her element in the world at times. Not quite helpless, but more like lost—getting her bearings. After all, it had taken her less than three days to pull together a functional life, without any identification, sure, but with a wardrobe, a place to stay, and even a job.

On that note, Brett still wasn't sure why he hadn't called the cops when she'd popped up with no explanation. If he hadn't been the one buying and preparing all the food, he'd have thought she'd drugged him. That was unlikely at best, and despite himself, Brett kind of liked having her around. Even the uncomfortable awkwardness that persisted between them was weirdly more pleasant than being alone, now that he had met her. In those rare moments when she confidently discussed literature and creativity, she shone, enchanting him.

The fact was, she hadn't tried to take advantage of him financially, and she hadn't stolen anything, not that there was much to take on either front. She hadn't even asked him for anything, other than help getting the job to pay him back. When he was with her, she felt alluringly familiar. And he'd written more since her arrival than he had in the months before.

Other than the bizarre circumstances behind her appearance, he was running out of reasons to keep her at such a distance. Her being unbelievably sexy didn't help him stay detached. As if to prove that point, Allie snaked her tongue out to capture a flake of salmon on her fork, wholly unaware of the effect she had.

"How was your day?" Brett asked. Distracting himself with conversation seemed like a good call.

Her face tilted toward him, and she froze. "It was fine," she said rapidly. Brett calmly kept her gaze. "How—how was yours?"

"It was okay. Got some work done." Her lips pressed lightly together, acknowledging his answer. He didn't want to talk about his work. Despite his lessening distrust, that was still off limits. He hated discussing works in progress with anyone anyway. "How're you liking waitressing?"

"It's very different for me." Silence.

Brett flaked off some more salmon. He had no idea what to talk about with her.

"Some of the customers are quite nice," Alexandra added.

"Are the others giving you any trouble?"

"I'm not as efficient as the other waitresses."

"People can be jerks. You shouldn't take it personally."

The corners of her lips pulled slightly up for a second, and she looked down. Apparently he'd struck a chord. Allie—*Alexandra*—twirled her fork in the veggies remaining on her plate.

Brett seized the opportunity to watch her. Her long hair still cascaded over her upper body, but it was pulled partially back in the clip he'd bought. Her tee shirt peeked through the deeply red locks.

Despite his earlier attempt, an impenetrable wall separated their seats at the dining table. He wanted to find a way to connect with her as more than strangers tossed together by implausible circumstance. He couldn't remember the last time she'd spoken without a direct question, except when it came to writing.

"So, listen, there's a great book I read a little while back." That got her attention, bringing her gaze back to him. "It's a translation, but I thought it might interest you, especially with your passion for literature."

"I would love to borrow it then, if you wouldn't mind."

"Of course." That wouldn't lead to spending more time with her. "Or we could, uh, we could read it together. After dinner." His grandparents had loved sitting together, reading. Even when he and Vicky had been too preoccupied to join them, their voices had echoed through their home, filling every nook and cranny, alternating depending on the book.

"Together?"

"Out loud. We could switch off, or I could…" Crazy was apparently the theme of the last few days. "I could read to you."

She smiled shyly and glanced down, then back at him. "What is it about?"

Brett smiled back. "It's a surprise."

After they'd finished eating, Brett insisted the dishes could wait. He'd clearly intrigued her, and he was excited to follow through, certain she would enjoy this story. He pulled *The Shadow of the Wind* off the shelf and ran his thumb automatically over the pages. Alexandra stood by the glass coffee table, watching him carefully, but without the tinge of anxiety that had previously thrummed through her body.

"Make yourself comfortable," he invited.

She curled on one end of the couch, wrapping her arms loosely around her waist. Brett settled near the other end so he didn't crowd her. She was riveted from the first sentence, as he had been. Just like the book's young protagonist, Brett fell deeply into the story as he read.

The end of the prologue freed him briefly from the book's spell. He glanced at Alexandra. He wasn't sure when, but her head had dropped to the back of the couch, and her eyes had closed. He couldn't really blame her. Her first few shifts must have been both mentally and physically exhausting.

Brett shut the book and placed it gently on the coffee table. He didn't want to leave her sleeping on the couch, so he stood beside her and said quietly, "Alexandra." When she didn't move, Brett leaned down to brush her shoulder. His hand rested on her impossibly soft hair. "Alexandra, Allie, wake up."

Her eyes fluttered open, and she smiled, slightly. Her rose-petal lips were inches from his, and she easily accepted his touch. Those green eyes watched him, luring him deeper even than the book had moments ago.

Brett's face hovered above her. Its simple lines were ornamented by the muted yet distinct curves of his lips. She wasn't certain why they drew her focus, but she didn't mind. Her lips parted on an inhale as she deliberated what to say, but the air was replaced by those beguiling curves, pressing against her lips, and her eyes closed again of their own accord. The gently shifting pressure didn't engulf her in flames the way some of her charges had described. Rather, it warmed her tenderly, and Allie rose toward the sensation, straightening from the couch.

He pulled a breath away, and Allie's eyes snapped open as her fingers flew to the tingling in her lips. Nothing lingered to explain the sensation. Brett's eyes caught the movement, and he stepped away.

"I'm sorry. I shouldn't have done that."

Allie couldn't move from her seat as her mind raced through the past minutes in an attempt to unscramble them. "Why did you?" The hypothetical idea of human passion wasn't novel to her. Many mimicked it for the pure enjoyment they claimed it brought—a deep connection to their bodies, pleasurable in part due to the perfection of one's partner. Allie was far from perfect.

"I couldn't help myself," he whispered. "I'm sorry."

At least in this one instance, Allie could be honest. "I didn't mind." The slip of his lips against hers had somehow spread the pleasant warmth beyond the point of contact, throughout her body.

Brett's body moved subtly nearer, before he stepped back with clenched fists. "I should let you get some sleep."

Chapter 10

Allie hadn't slept much. Between attempting to bind the sensation of Brett's kiss within her memory and failing to construct an alternate, more pleasing continuation that had persistently eluded her imagination, she had lain awake for hours.

I couldn't help myself, he had said. Had magic intervened? If it had, then why? And why had he stopped? Had she done something wrong? Had the experience been intolerably horrible for him?

Allie forced herself to breathe deeply and regarded her reflection. It was time, once again, to struggle with containing her hair before leaving for work. Even in the mortal realm, it swished comfortingly around her, but the unrestricted movement wasn't allowed in her new position. Using the brush to guide the locks, she gathered her hair at the apex of her head then stretched the band, slipping it over and around, then twisting it and repeating to ensure it held.

This left her hair slightly more restrained yet still cascading over her back. If she twisted now, it would fly even more. She left the first band in and braided the flowing thickness, securing it again. If she spun fast enough, the result could almost be used as a weapon, but the lines were clean—nearly austere, leaving her features exposed. Presumably the diner's clientele wouldn't pay sufficient attention to be put off. She had already selected a muted yet feminine top, for added confidence after last night. The charcoal fabric crossed over her chest and fluttered at her shoulders.

It wasn't that early, but there were no noises in the house other than from her own movements. Allie slipped out as quietly as possible, particularly relieved that she didn't have to rely on Brett to reach the diner.

The street was quiet, and the sunshine warmed her through air still tinged with a chill. The walk finally cleared her scrambled thoughts. She needed to focus on her shift and then on solving the mystery behind her current state. That was all that mattered.

"Alexandra!" Nate, the artist, greeted when she walked into the diner.

Allie couldn't help but smile. At least one person was happy to see her. Nate had been spending hours at the diner each day, though this time he had chosen a booth. Her smile faltered when his eyes narrowed, taking in her hairstyle.

He soon shook his head and continued as though that moment hadn't happened. "I have something to show you."

He pulled something packaged loosely in brown paper from beside him. Allie stepped closer. He slid the rectangle to the edge of the table, visibly bouncing his knee.

"What is it?"

"A new painting. I spent almost all night working on it."

Since Nate hadn't been one of her charges, Allie had no knowledge of his work or skill. Was he a classical painter? A post-modernist one? Her curiosity was piqued, though she didn't know how she was expected to respond. The rectangle's longest side was about the length of her arm. Should she unwrap it? Wait for him to do so? Why had he chosen to share it with her?

"Go ahead, open it." His knee finally stilled as her fingers moved over the wrapping, cautiously lifting it away from the work below.

The image caught her breath. A realistic depiction featured a sole figure amid a natural background with trees and a river flowing from distant mountains. Peculiarly, the figure stood nude, covered in nothing but a draped cloth held at her chest and the red hair cascading around her. He'd captured her adeptly, yet with sultry nuances in her expression that Allie was certain her face had never held. This was a woman who'd known passion—the mythic Eve of human stories, after she had tasted the forbidden fruit. Peripherally, Allie noticed a bit apple lying at the base of the nearest tree. Apparently her interpretation hadn't been entirely unfounded.

"Do you hate it?" Nate's voice fought through her mind's haze.

"Of course not. It's quite skilled. But, why would you paint this?" She couldn't look at him. The intimacy of the painted gaze was penetrating.

"You inspired me."

The simple statement finally drew her gaze from the canvas. She had literally inspired so many, yet none had been compelled to include her in the resulting work, entirely oblivious to her existence. Her presence and effect weren't intended to be noticed. Now that they had been, she herself had no words.

"Are you just going to stand there all day or are you going to clock in?" Kristie commented breezing past the booth. She took a couple steps back and stopped, staring at the painting. "Wow, Nate."

"Kristie."

"Looks like you found your muse."

Allie stiffened automatically at the words. Some latent magic may very well have affected the artist, but the waitress couldn't possibly know the truth behind her statement. Kristie spun away, racing to the kitchen.

Belatedly, the acerbity of Kristie's words struck her, and pieces pulled into a whole in her mind. Nate had been the one to comment on Kristie's behavior on Allie's first day. "You were involved with her," she stated without judgment. Even her peers occasionally had difficulty maintaining emotional equilibrium after sharing passion. From the stories she knew, for humans it was significantly worse.

"That's not why I painted this. I haven't finished a painting in so long, and this one came so easily…" He trailed off, staring after Kristie.

"It is a beautiful painting," Allie acknowledged. Male artists had long histories of relationships with a myriad of women who caught their eyes. She knew there was nothing more than imagination, and perhaps a touch of magic, behind this painting, but Kristie couldn't, and the mortal was obviously upset. It was somewhat deserved, after her unwarranted antagonism, but Allie couldn't bring herself to ignore the blonde's obvious pain. "Excuse me," she murmured and followed the waitress.

Kristie rounded on her the moment she entered the back room. "You *slept* with him?! What, Brett wasn't enough for you? Does he even know?"

Slept? Allie would have expected accusations of a more intimate nature, but regardless, the false assumption had to be addressed. "No, I've never… Not with either of them, in fact."

"Yeah, right," Kristie sneered. "He used to paint me too, you know."

"It's not like that. I had no knowledge of the painting until he showed it to me." Allie maintained an even pitch to her voice. The truth behind her words would surely pierce through Kristie's wounded rage.

"You can't even own up to it, can you? Gotta maintain that perfect-little-innocent-angel act."

"She's telling the truth." Nate's voice spun both women around. Allie was left squarely between the mortals, and she hastily stepped back.

Kristie's shoulders squared, and her chin lifted. "Like I'll believe you."

"You didn't believe me, that's why we…" Nate stuffed his hands into the pockets of his trousers. "I've painted many women, Kristie. And men. I generally don't sleep with any of them. Alexandra didn't even pose for me."

"You never painted me like that." Tears added shine to her eyes and thickened her voice.

Allie snatched an apron and order pad and left as quickly as possible. She busied herself with refilling coffees and wiping down the bar.

Nate exited the kitchen first. He rewrapped the painting and approached Allie, who paused in rolling silverware sets into napkins. "I didn't mean to hurt her."

"I wouldn't have thought so."

"Will you take the painting?"

"You don't want to show it?" It was beautifully done, more masterfully than the work of many of her past charges. Not everyone possessed skill to match the inspiration. Then again, she had no frame of reference to compare it with his other work.

"Kristie doesn't understand. Art, this intimacy, it isn't the same as in life."

Allie nodded. "This is a fantasy to which you gave my face." It couldn't have required true intimacy, because they simply didn't share that.

"Amazing, how you synthesize that into words. Effortlessly. I can't do that. Maybe that's why… Well, you don't need to hear that."

"You express yourself differently, but no less effectively."

Nate sighed, tawny eyes seeking secrets in her face. "How is it you just gave me another idea when I've been empty for so long?"

Allie couldn't answer, but she didn't have to.

"Please, take the painting." His lips pulled to the side despite the sadness in his eyes. "Maybe someday it'll even be worth something."

"It's worth something now."

His lips tightened against each other. Gone was the easygoing calm she had already grown accustomed to seeing. He lifted the canvas onto the bar and tapped it twice. "I'll see you tomorrow."

After tossing some bills onto his table, he gathered his things and left. Kristie still hadn't emerged. A group of young men entered the diner, requiring Allie's attention. She slipped the painting behind the bar, tucking it behind a box of sugar packets for safety, and headed toward them.

Kissing Alexandra the night before had done nothing to improve Brett's focus. Erotic images of them together flashed through his mind almost nonstop. Maybe his only choice was to flush them from his system onto the page. He certainly couldn't expect his mystery guest to bring them to life.

He'd stayed silent as she got ready for work and left. What would he have seen in her eyes if he hadn't? He'd chosen the cowardly way of avoiding the rationality of the morning after. His mind preferred to play in the possibilities of the night before.

There were countless options for bodies entwining in slick, heated passion, and in his mind right now, each one featured Alexandra. In the privacy of his own mind, a man could enjoy a series of sensual nighttime encounters.

But what if the fantasies turned out to be anything but a dream?

"Missing person? Why the hell's that one of ours?" Pete barked. He'd been waking up exhausted, drained from the erotic dreams he sure as hell wouldn't trade for a cheery demeanor. They could take it. "Evidence of foul play?"

"No, sir." DETECTIVE2 looked nervous. Pete's tone wouldn't have done that. The younger man glanced at his partner. "We thought you'd want to see this one."

Pete grunted. "Why's that?"

DETECTIVE3 chimed in. "Her last known location is, uh, well."

"Well?"

"Your house. Sir."

"My house?" He hadn't had any guests in weeks. Pete strode toward the board they'd started but stopped short. There, in the victim's slot, was the woman of his dreams. Literally.

It wasn't brilliant, but it was an okay start—a woman slipping into the detective's bedroom without his realization for nightly bouts of sensual exercise, only to disappear with barely a trace. It'd be quite the trick to unravel. And he could start with the dreams, channeling all the impropriety in his imagination into productivity. Writing so explicitly would be new for him, but at least he had an abundance of material in his mind. And if he wrote about it for his book, it wasn't inappropriate. Right?

By the time Alexandra opened the front door, Brett had nearly a dozen pages filled with fantasies that could only barely be excused by his profession. Imagining being with her, seeing her in the lingerie he'd bought just days ago, exploring every inch of her impossibly white skin, had had an uncomfortable side effect.

He wouldn't have been thrilled with her seeing any of his drafts, but these pages definitely couldn't ever come before her eyes. He saved the file to his password-protected draft folder and closed it, then turned off the screen for good measure.

Maybe he could sneak into a cold shower. He rose from the desk chair and headed out of his office, opening the door right as Alexandra passed. *Perfect.*

She stopped, eyes widening in surprise. Her hair was pulled tightly away from her face, emphasizing her improbably green eyes and the slightly parted lips whose timid softness he couldn't forget. His gaze dropped away, unintentionally trailing over her lush figure, until he saw the package in her hands.

"What've you got there?" he asked, seizing on the innocuous topic.

"Oh, it's…a painting."

"Oh yeah? Slow day at work?"

"One of the artists who spends time at the diner gave it to me." She shifted her weight to one hip.

"Nick? or Neil? I've seen him around." And he'd given her his art.

"Nate."

"You guys been getting close?" This was starting to resemble an interrogation.

"He's kind. It's a skillful painting."

He could have sworn he saw a faint blush cover her cheeks. "Am I allowed to see it?" He was definitely pushing the limits of polite behavior. His grandmother would have been appalled, but Alexandra had gotten under his skin. She'd kissed him back just last night, and today another man was giving her gifts. What exactly was she doing at the diner? The hours of fantasizing and writing weren't helping him react rationally.

"Of—of course." She contemplated the package in her hand then held it out to him. "Please. I would like to change, after work, if you wouldn't mind."

Brett took the proffered edge. Alexandra opened her mouth to speak but apparently reconsidered. She let go of the painting and disappeared into her room. *His* bedroom.

Brett shut the door to his office and took the painting to the living room, so he could see it under natural light. He unwrapped the loose paper, letting it fall to the floor. Apparently he wasn't the only one fantasizing about Alexandra. Though for all he knew, this might not be a fantasy.

What had he been thinking? Nearly obsessing about a woman he barely knew, who couldn't possibly be as innocent as she seemed. The painted version watched him with sensuality that rivaled the heat of his written words.

The draping in her hands mimicked the blanket she had grabbed when he'd first seen her, loosely covering the most intimate body parts while revealing tantalizing expanses of skin.

"I didn't know."

Brett's gaze flew to the live subject of the painting. She hadn't changed so much as let her hair down and removed her shoes and socks.

"About the painting," she explained. "I didn't know."

"It's beautiful."

"It's fantasy."

He trailed his eyes down her body, then to the painting. The knowledge in the image's eyes wasn't reflected in her own. But even if the painting had no more connection to reality than the pages on his computer, that was cold comfort. He couldn't stand having only as much of her as this other man.

Could he really blame the artist for using Alexandra the same way he had? Not rationally. The roiling jealousy was foreign to him.

Brett lowered the painting to the coffee table, beside the book he hadn't replaced on its shelf. Didn't he have more of a connection with her than a distanced observation transformed into a fantasy?

Chapter 11

Allie didn't know what to expect. She couldn't think of an acceptable reason not to show him the painting, so she had, despite fearing an overreaction similar to Kristie's. Perhaps that was presumptuous, and he was unaffected? That seemed worse. There had to be a means of diverting his attention.

"Have you eaten?" she ventured. Other than a sandwich at the diner, she hadn't consumed much, and Brett seemed to enjoy preparing meals.

"Not yet." He didn't move.

She hadn't done anything other than accept a gift pressed upon her, but that didn't seem to matter to the humans. The book he had begun reading to her rested before him. She had been too exhausted to remember much, but it had begun masterfully. Having him read to her had felt comfortable and safe, as though she was a welcome part of his life, but they had yet to discuss the night before. Would they? Was she expected to ignore it? He had kissed *her*!

Allie fought the desire to sink her teeth into her bottom lip. She had to maintain control over herself. Succumbing to her frustrations was likely what had led to her entrapment in this realm in the first place.

"Could I help you prepare something?"

Finally, he moved, walking stiffly toward the kitchen and leaving the troublesome painting behind. "What're you in the mood for? I mean, for dinner."

She crossed to the tiles that marked the kitchen's boundary. "Your choices have been impeccable."

"How about baked pasta?"

It wasn't something served at the diner, so Allie had no frame of reference. "I trust your judgment." *With regards to food, anyway.*

She fought to maintain a blank expression when he turned around. "Please, have a seat. You must be tired after being on your feet all day." It was like a switch had been flipped, returning Brett to the role of a faultless host.

Her feet did ache, though. Allie settled gratefully on one of the chairs beside the empty counter.

Brett extracted various ingredients and dishware from around the kitchen. Once he had set a filled pot on the stove, he asked, "So are you working tomorrow?"

"From nine to three." The day afterward, she wasn't scheduled for a shift. Her body would relish the break.

"Nice, you have the evening off?"

Obviously. "Yes."

Brett rinsed the vegetables he had selected and brought them to the counter in front of her, along with a knife and a rectangular board.

"I would be happy to assist you," she reminded.

"Do you know how to cook?"

"Not at all, actually." Yet another basic function of human life with which she had no experience. It shouldn't have disturbed her—she *wasn't* human—but appearing incompetent around Brett bothered her.

"Well, chopping's pretty easy." He slid everything toward her, maintaining his grip on the blade. "This knife is really sharp though, so be careful."

Allie repositioned the ingredients before her as Brett rounded the counter. He flipped the knife's direction, holding the handle out to her. At his encouraging nod, Allie carefully wrapped her fingers around the manmade material. Brett didn't let go, raising his other hand to reposition her grip. He stood beside her elbow, closer than they had been since the night before. She trained her gaze firmly on the knife. He reached in front of her to place a green vegetable on the board.

"So with the zucchini, you want to discard the ends." She held the oblong shape with her left hand, placed the knife atop it, and pushed. The knife barely pressed into the green. "Rest the knife against the zucchini and move it forward to slice through the skin," Brett corrected. "Then back toward yourself and down. It'll cut right through."

Allie brought the blade forward as he said, pleased to see it pierce the vegetable, then lowered it slowly as she moved her wrist back. The result was a break more than a slice. Brett moved around her, placing one hand over hers on the knife and shifting her hold on the zucchini away from the blade with the other. The back of Allie's chair barely separated them, and the warmth of his body seeped into her. Her lungs forgot how to function.

Brett silently but deftly directed her hand in brisk, downward motions. The blade hit the board with an even rhythm. Halfway through, he paused, removing his hands. "You try it." He still stood behind her.

The blade is sharp, Alexandra. Pay attention! She replicated the motion he had demonstrated, dismayed to see the resulting slices weren't as even as his.

"Good," he said regardless and walked back to the stove.

A rushing hiss filled the air as he emptied something into the pot. Allie reached for the second zucchini. Brett busied himself with the other ingredients. By the time Allie had chopped all the vegetables into acceptably small pieces, he had placed pale yellow tubes into an open glass rectangle and covered them in sauces he had mixed. He stirred in the vegetables then concealed the mixture under a layer of cheese.

With the pasta baking in the oven, Brett had no way to occupy his hands. Allie watched him silently. He'd been an idiot to demonstrate the way he had, but it had been impossible to resist. He'd never considered cooking an intimate activity, but clearly with the right companion it could be.

"How was your day?" she asked politely.

Filled with fantasies. "Pretty productive." Her nod ended with her chin dipping, face tilting down. Brett came around the island. "Allie." Her name came out hoarsely. Her eyes returned to him. Brett swallowed. A flaming lock had drifted forward, over her brow. Brett's hand lifted to brush it back before his mind caught up.

The barstool on which she sat was high enough that he barely had to bend to taste her. Her lips moved pliantly against his, chin tilting to match his angle. Brett brushed her mouth in a succession of soft kisses then shifted to the point below her ear. He brushed her hair further aside, and Allie arched toward him as his mouth trailed down the side of her neck.

Her skin was softer than he'd imagined. Her scent reminded him of flowers, though he couldn't place which. Brett flicked his tongue out, and she gasped almost imperceptibly.

But her hands didn't move to touch him. He pulled back, exhaling, and she shivered in response. Damn, how he wanted to keep going. He forced himself to step back.

Her parted lips had darkened from the pressure of his. Her eyebrows drew together over rounded eyes. He didn't know what to make of the hesitance or confusion. "You don't have to do this." Her expression didn't change. Brett ran his hand through his own hair then dropped it to the island. "I don't want you to feel like… You don't owe me anything."

Her tongue darted out between her lips before they closed. He clenched the fist she couldn't see.

"I don't understand," she admitted softly.

The lost innocence contrasted starkly in his mind with the sultry knowledge of the painting, the confidence of his Vixen character. He had to be more clear. "You don't have to do anything you don't want to, anything you don't like."

She continued to watch him, the uncertainty plainly evident in the crooked line of her brows.

"Have you ever been with anyone?" Brett asked bluntly.

She stilled and moments later shook her head. Quicksand sucked at his stomach. Was he taking advantage of her?

"Do you like it when I kiss you?" Such a simple question, with an excruciatingly important answer.

Her gaze dipped for an instant, but then she breathed, "Yes."

The concern that had churned within him eased. Brett fought himself not to act on the information.

"Do you?"

Her timid question caught him off guard. In today's world, how could she be so incredibly innocent? He could barely keep his hands off her, and she wasn't even sure that he liked kissing her. Brett closed the distance between them, gently cupping her jaw. His thumb brushed her cheek. She blinked slowly, and her lips parted just barely. He had to take it slow.

But he wasn't a saint.

Her lips shifted softly under his, mimicking his movements. His tongue traced her lips then delved into her mouth. She responded hesitantly to the motion, stilling before her tongue delicately joined his. He ran his hands down her arms, intertwining their fingers. His thumbs traced patterns in her palms as he savored her mouth.

Beeping from the oven timer jerked Allie back. Brett froze, returning to reality. Allie twisted, searching for the source of the sound. "Hey. It's okay." She looked back to him, and tension dropped from her shoulders. Brett glanced back at her lips, forcing himself to let go, and headed to the oven.

The baked pasta was delicious, its varying textures mingling in Allie's mouth. The same flavors simultaneously played within Brett's, which was a strange thought to have.

Her clothes pressed uncomfortably against the heightened sensitivity of her skin.

Was this passion—thrilling at his touch? Or was it an inevitability borne of their prolonged proximity?

His scent and taste had invaded her senses. Was that the attraction of which humans wrote? The descriptions of naked, writhing bodies hadn't made as distinct an impression on her as that brief moment with this one man.

What had they just done?

Their encounter had remained relatively chaste, insofar as she understood. What did that mean for her continued stay? It was entirely too complex.

Even after the previous night, she hadn't anticipated the soft pleasure that had thrummed through her with him close, his lips playing over hers and down her neck briefly before he had pulled away.

She still didn't understand why he had. Her fear that she'd been unacceptably maladroit hadn't matched his subsequent words. Or him kissing her again.

"How is it?" His warm, clear eyes studied her.

Allie wanted to disappear under the soft scrutiny. Being noticed had its downsides. "It's wonderful." She slipped another gooey mix of cheese and vegetables into her mouth.

She longed to be closer to him, which made no sense. The previous night's lack of sleep and the day's heightened emotions had drained her. She needed to think, away from his perplexing proximity.

Brett tossed a stress ball between his hands, staring at the protected pages on his screen. Allie had declined to spend time reading after dinner, claiming fatigue. Maybe she'd really been tired, but her uncertainty during their provocative makeout session made him think there was more to it.

Of course, his desire had to take a back seat to her innocence. Instead he tortured himself by rereading the heated scenes he'd written. The sensuality of the pages couldn't compare to the unexpected sweetness of reality. Allie was nothing like Pete's mystery, but both women were equally inscrutable.

Chapter 12

Friday's shift had been her shortest thus far, but Allie was still exhausted. Her and Wanda's scheduled times at the diner had barely overlapped, so she had spent the majority of her time overseeing the patrons alone. Nate hadn't come in at all, depriving her of a distraction during lulls.

Now an inevitable conversation with Brett awaited her inside, though she continued to feel thoroughly off-kilter. Furthermore, all of these interpersonal, *mortal,* issues were supposed to be irrelevant.

She longed to fill up the large basin in his bathroom and spend some time soaking in the water.

Silence greeted her in the entryway of Brett's home. A flash of unexpected color in the living room drew her attention. *The painting.* Its presence stole the momentary, false promise of peace. Allie strode to the low table and quickly rewrapped the canvas in the discarded paper. She took it to the room she continued to occupy and searched for a secluded spot. She decided on the floor of the closet, allowing garments to drape over the painting to obscure it from view. It had already caused more trouble than she could have predicted.

Then again, absolutely nothing about this assignment had gone as anticipated.

Brett hadn't emerged from his office. Perhaps she could actually attempt a bath, though first she would have to discern how to prevent the water from seeping out of the hole in the bottom of the basin.

Twenty minutes later, Allie watched water collect and spread over the white surface. She adjusted the temperature then locked both doors. With her hair braided, the octopus clip could secure it well enough that it shouldn't slip into the water. She perched on the basin's edge and swirled her hand in the gathering pool. It wouldn't be quite like the secluded natural lake she could have enjoyed had she been in the fae realm, but she could imagine, and the warm water would hopefully be sufficiently soothing.

The water embraced her body, caressing each swell and crevice as Allie lowered herself into the basin. She left the glass door open, allowing the steam to escape rather than attacking her head. Droplets beaded on her uncovered skin nevertheless. The water shifted only with her breath. Allie shut her eyes, allowing the warmth to ease the soreness of her mortal form.

Her mind drifted back to the night before, relishing the memory of Brett's touch. She still couldn't imagine what would have happened had he not stopped. Would his mouth have trailed lower, down her neck and then even further? Would the cloth that separated their bodies have been discarded? Where else would he have touched her? And would she have then, in turn, explored his body? Not the stone replica of a master, but the vital heat of an original.

Or would Brett have all too quickly been disappointed by her shape, or lack of experience?

Sighing, Allie rose from the cooling water. In a motion she barely thought about anymore, she pulled the purple towel from its hook and wrapped it around her dripping body. A tap of her foot on the silver plug set the water rushing down the resulting opening.

Back in the bedroom, she dried the parts of her body the towel couldn't otherwise reach. A flick of her fingers sent her braid uncoiling down her back. She set the clip on one of the small tables beside the bed.

A soft tapping sounded from the opposite side of the door that led to the hallway. Allie snatched up the discarded towel, re-wrapping it securely before stepping to the door to inch it open.

Brett's gaze stilled momentarily above the top of the towel. The beginning traces of a beard covered his jaw, and his hair lay disheveled. Not long ago she would have been repelled by his unkempt appearance, but she knew now it wasn't, in his case, a sign of disregard for hygiene.

"Hey," he eventually said.

"Hi."

"I was wondering if you'd like to go out tonight, for dinner. With me."

"Out?"

"Yeah, we could go to a nice restaurant, spend some time getting to know each other." His lips slipped into a diagonal smile. "You could try some better cooking than mine."

Her lips curled of their own volition. "You're more than adept at cooking."

"Is that a yes?"

Was it? Was there some hidden mortal meaning behind the invitation? How much of herself could she truly share with him? A slight pinch between his brows prompted her to decide. "Yes."

This was either the best or worst idea he'd ever had. Allie had braided a complex pattern into her hair that somehow still left locks spilling over her back and shoulders. She'd chosen a purple top that showcased her flawless skin and draped over her breasts, pairing it with a black skirt. Sweetly beautiful but still extraordinarily sexy.

Brett sipped his scotch. Allie twirled the straw in her rum smoothie.

"So."

Her hand stilled, then dropped beneath the table. "So?"

"Where did you learn to love books so much?"

"What do you mean?"

"You do like books, right?"

"Good ones," she answered with an earnest nod.

"That's a tautology."

Her lips curved. "Yes, I suppose it is." She paused. "I've spent the majority of my life surrounded by writers and artists."

"Really?" Brett settled back into his chair. Finally, it seemed, he'd learn more about her.

"You wouldn't believe the range of works I've watched be created."

"Have you ever written, or created, anything yourself?"

"No." Her eyes danced over the table between them before returning to him. "And yourself? What prompted you to become a writer?"

Brett reached for his scotch. Allie mirrored his movement, sipping her drink. "I spent a lot of time when I was younger trying to figure things out: people, situations; seeing people's motivations and how far some would go for the promise of a reward. I learned the power of words pretty early on. So I guess it was inevitable."

"So now you script your own puzzles."

"Something like that." The arrival of their food saved him from elaborating.

Allie smiled up at the waitress. She seemed instinctively comfortable in the elegant surroundings of the restaurant. She handled every piece of the table setting with a casual ease that betrayed familiarity with the formality somewhat at odds with her desire to work as a waitress.

"How is your writing going?"

Brett bristled at the question despite himself. He couldn't shake the feeling that she was weirdly invested in his writing, but that was ridiculous. Besides, his writing was a huge part of him. He'd been the one to open the door on getting to know each other better. Even if he'd really meant getting to know *her* better. "It's in the beginning, floating around stages, as I pin down a set of characters and a path."

"You're evaluating ideas?"

"I think I've hit on a decent premise. Working on untangling it, finding the right thread." He wasn't big on planning out every detail before writing, but he liked to have a general sense of the story.

"Are you waiting to be inspired?"

"More like, picking through the inspiration until I can see where I'm going." Allie watched him intently. No one other than Vicky had been this interested in his writing since their grandparents. Even Sean mostly cared about the end result, which suited Brett just fine. But Allie's attentiveness was nice. She seemed more interested in where his writing was now than the abstract potential of a finished, sellable book. Not that he could ever show her the steamy scenes he'd written. "How's the lobster?"

She glanced at the plate, following his redirection. "Surprising. I didn't expect the texture and flavors to meld like this."

"So you like it?"

She smiled and nodded. "Would you like to try some?"

Slipping a morsel between his lips would bring her closer, angled over the table. Or he could try the lingering taste in her mouth. "You enjoy it."

"How is your…?"

"The steak? It's great, cooked perfectly." He paused. "Would you like a taste?"

Her lips rounded for a moment. "That's all right. Thank you, though."

Brett stabbed a roasted piece of zucchini. Allie dipped a piece of lobster into the little pot of melted butter, sliding it against the rounded edge before bringing it to her mouth. Butter glistened on her lip before her tongue flicked out. When had he become so stereotypically single-minded?

"So, besides books and art, what kinds of things interest you?"

Allie reached for her drink before answering. "Music." Her voice lilted up questioningly.

"Kind of counts as an art, doesn't it?"

"Well, I don't quite know, then. I suppose my life had been fairly consumed." Her expression fell as it tended to when her past came up.

There was obviously something she kept from him. Maybe he was being an idiot, but the possibility of it being threatening or malicious no longer struck him as likely.

She recovered quickly to resume the thread of their conversation. "What about yourself? Other than writing and cooking, and rescuing damsels in distress." She stilled at the easy teasing of her last words, as if afraid she'd crossed a line.

Brett smiled at the fairytale notion. "Believe it or not, I don't come across distressed damsels all that often."

Her eyes sparked. "So you relished the opportunity to play hero?"

"Maybe it just took a special damsel to catch my attention. Not that you're all that great at playing the distressed role."

A startled laugh escaped her. "How do you mean?"

"You just don't really strike me as helpless."

She sobered at the observation, features straightening into an unaffected yet alert state.

"I guess the best damsels never are," he added. He'd never before realized how true that was.

Allie twirled her fork in her risotto with delicately flushed cheeks. "You didn't answer my question," she pointed out.

He traced their conversation backwards, searching for the lost thread. Damsels, heroes… Hobbies. "Running, basketball sometimes." Not as much as he should lately. "Recently, hosting a beautiful, enchanting houseguest."

Allie froze as a blush filled her cheeks, and then a timid smile stretched across her face, making the somewhat cheesy line entirely worth it.

Brett stopped the car in the driveway because the garage felt wrong after the nice restaurant. Allie had been silent on the ride home, as though the awkwardness between them that had slowly fallen away over dinner had begun rebuilding. He offered her his hand, helping her out of the car, then steered her to the front door. On a date, he'd probably have made a move. But was this a date? The rules couldn't possibly be the same with a woman who was staying in your house. Taking things more slowly was the smarter choice. Forget the fact that they'd already made out.

A kiss on the porch was supposed to end the evening, anyway, and he didn't want the night to end, even if it wasn't actually a date. He unlocked the door and gestured for her to precede him.

Brett's voice coiled through the living room as he read. Allie sat quietly on the other end of the couch, unwilling to disturb the story built by the author's words and through which Brett's voice guided her.

Their dinner had been both delectable and entertaining, but she had been further destabilized by Brett's conscientious courteousness throughout the evening. The intensity of his nearly uninterrupted attention had prickled along her skin and painted over her. Even among her own kind, she had rarely been the recipient of such uninterrupted yet unthreatening focus.

The steady rhythm of Brett's voice stopped, and the contrast of the silence was staggering.

"I'm not sure how to pronounce this word," he said. "Maybe you could help me."

She shifted closer without comment, leaning past his shoulder to see the word above his finger. "None?" She twisted her head away from the page to look at him. Clearly, she had misunderstood. "You weren't certain how to pronounce 'none'?"

Brett's eyes narrowed with his smile before his lips touched hers. Two soft brushes later, he pulled away, and his arm landed gently around her shoulders. He resumed reading nonchalantly, apparently content with the results of his trap.

Allie sat frozen. The proximity wasn't unpleasant, but it suffused her with a keen awareness of every point of connection between them. His fingers traced unintelligible patterns on the exposed surface below her sleeve. His breathing vibrated through her other arm, captured against his side, as his voice regained its rhythm. Their thighs pressed against each other. The steady warmth of his mortal body soaked into her. She didn't want to move away but couldn't relax or focus on the words beyond his tone. An unexplained tingling afflicted even parts of her body he didn't touch.

At the next break in the story, the book drifted shut. She turned to him. Did he want to end the evening? His fingers stilled on her arm. She briefly glimpsed the golden sparks in his eyes before his gaze fell to her lips. His arm dragged slightly off her shoulder to her back as he angled his body toward her. His other hand lifted to play at the juncture of her ear and jaw. Her eyes drifted shut momentarily, opening as she inhaled, breathing him in as he kissed her.

His arm moved from her back to her head, tangling through her hairstyle. He didn't let go when he ended the kiss. He had bathed before dinner, and her every breath was saturated with his surprisingly pleasant scent, fruity and fresh. She twisted her upper body to match the angle of his and followed the motion through to link their lips again. Brett's fingers flexed in her hair.

His tongue traced over her bottom lip, and Allie opened her mouth, letting it slip in. He led her in a dance she had never imagined, angling her head to deepen the kiss. His fingers drifted from her jaw, down her arm, grazing her breast before stilling over her ribs. Allie arched into his touch, searching for something she couldn't pinpoint. She lifted her arm, flattening her palm over the outside of his shoulder. The feel of the pliant firmness curled her fingers around him.

His lips jumped to her neck, fluttering over her skin before his tongue flicked out. Her head tilted back, and her muscles contracted on their own, sending a small motion through her upper body and further curving her fingers. Brett's breath skimmed the dampness on her neck.

He straightened away from her, lifting his hand from her side. Allie dropped her hand to her lap. His other hand untangled from her hair, landing on her shoulder. His thumb moved over her collar. He was still close enough for her to see his jaw clench. Allie looked away.

Brett's lips brushed her forehead. "We should stop."

She glanced up in time to see him swallow. What could she say to that? Her hands sank into the couch as she lifted away from him and his touch.

"Allie."

The familiar nickname on his lips cut through her. She faced him, striving in her stance for the closed detachment that had so recently been entirely habitual for her. "Thank you for dinner, and everything."

"Hey." He shot up from the couch, grabbing her hand.

Her false bravado crumbled at the edges, and her own jaw clenched.

He stepped closer.

Why did she still want him to kiss her after his rejection?

He intertwined their fingers. "The last thing I want is to stop."

But you did.

"But I'm not going to—like this, on the couch. You deserve better."

The sentiment sunk through her confusion without dispelling it. "Good night, then," she half asked.

Brett stepped closer still, leaving the merest distance between them. Allie tilted her face up to maintain eye contact. His lips captured hers for no more than a few heartbeats, before he let go and stepped away. "Good night."

Chapter 13

I've always been fascinated by various mythologies," Brett said, setting down the backpack and picnic basket he'd brought for them to one of his favorite hideaways. Allie had the day off, and he'd seized the opportunity to take her on a proper yet fun date. "So many different cultures which ingrained these crafted stories into their realities, independently, and yet so many of them have common threads. It reveals so much about humanity, human nature."

He held out his hand for the blanket Allie had insisted on carrying from the car. She didn't notice, enthralled by their luscious surroundings. At least, it seemed, he'd chosen well. This small park was only about an hour from his place, but it didn't offer many amenities other than its breathtaking view of the mountains, so it was frequently empty, even on a Saturday.

He took the plush blanket from her hands, and Allie startled but smiled shyly. Brett considered ducking down for a kiss, but he didn't want to disturb the easy amiability they'd found today.

"What if your mythology was real?" she asked, helping him spread the blanket.

"What do you mean?"

"Well, as you said, there were common threads among different cultures' myths. What if that was because there was truth behind the ideas? Even if they were ultimately altered."

Brett contemplated as they settled on the ground. "So, what? Nothing in our world can function without the interference of mystical, invisible powers? Isn't that just shirking responsibility for our own reality?"

Piercing green looked unflinchingly back at him. As off-kilter as she seemed about some basic things, it was obvious a sharp mind was enveloped in her stunning looks. It hardly seemed fair.

"Everything has its role to play. Seedlings sprout only where water, sunshine, and earth come together in a perfect combination of conditions. Some may be tougher, more resilient than others, but they nevertheless remain dependent on the right conditions, which are ultimately created through outside assistance. Why couldn't that support come from nymphs, or fairies, or sprites? Or others—entities from beyond this realm whose existence is defined by watching over and assisting mortals."

Hearing her talk about it, it almost seemed possible. "Wouldn't they get bored?" A smile spread across her face. "I mean, considering how ungrateful most people are, it sounds like an awfully frustrating role, for any creature with its own mind. And if they're mindless, they might as well be just the sun or the rain."

She laughed outright, looking out over the mountains. Brett couldn't help smiling at the chiming sound that quickly dissipated into their surroundings. "Perhaps you have a point," she acceded, still grinning.

Brett pulled the juice and glasses he'd brought from his grandmother's basket. For all the beauty around them, nothing compared to Allie's, but he hadn't brought her here to ravish her. And he really enjoyed talking to her when she wasn't skittish. He handed her a glass, stilling in the face of her joyful gaze. Her eyes dipped away first, breaking the spell. Brett allowed himself a moment to watch her, seated with her legs outstretched before her, torso slightly arched from the pressure of leaning back onto one hand as the other brought the glass to her lips, still touched by the remnants of a smile. Her hair fell all the way to the blanket, gleaming in the sunshine.

"So," he cleared his throat, "I brought the book and cards to entertain you."

"Cards?"

"Playing cards." A blank glance greeted the elaboration. He shouldn't have been surprised. Her unambiguous clarity seemed to be limited to philosophy and the arts, not the intricacies of daily reality. "Guess we'll start with the cards, then." He took them out of their pack, shuffling on autopilot. Too bad he was too much of a gentleman to suggest strip poker.

Allie's hand snaked out when she glimpsed a second seven land atop the pile. Brett groaned with a smile as she collected the stack of cards. He had smiled at her frequently today, but she didn't tire of seeing it. Their majestic surroundings belied the casualness of their activity, sprawled on the ground playing games. It was surprisingly enjoyable.

"Maybe we should play War, instead," Brett suggested, spreading his three remaining cards with his fingers.

"Is it more difficult?" They had begun by playing a rather simple game called "Go Fish," before switching to this one, which relied primarily on instinct. Their hands had brushed more than a few times in their attempts to slap the piled cards, but the exhilaration of the game prevented the touch from morphing into anything else. As a matter of fact, Brett had courteously refrained from touching her all day. Otherwise, though, the day had been thoroughly enjoyable. Allie flipped another card onto the blanket between them.

"No. In fact there's no strategy at all. It's purely based on luck." He flipped his card onto the pile. A jack. Allie added hers. An ace. His last two cards landed swiftly on top. "So I might actually have a chance at winning," he teased good-naturedly.

Allie stifled a chuckle. "Whatever you would like." She placed down the stack in her hands.

"Are you hungry?"

She paused before replying. Brett had said only that he wanted to spend the day with her over their light breakfast. She had no idea what else he had brought with them. She could easily subsist on the juice, if necessary, if that meant they didn't have to leave. Here, in the natural beauty and away from the rest of the mortal realm, she didn't feel quite as out of place. She was fairly certain he was also enjoying himself. "I wouldn't mind staying here for a while longer."

"Who said anything about leaving?" With a mischievous smile, he flipped open part of the basket's lid. As he withdrew items, Allie gathered the cards to make room. Containers of various sizes soon covered the expanse between them. Brett opened two of them, revealing a sandwich in each. "Roast beef or turkey?" he asked, holding out both in her direction.

He had gone through so much trouble, preparing everything. *Just for me.* It was unimaginable. "Up to you," she demurred politely.

"Lady's choice."

Thankfully, her time at the diner had familiarized her with many basic mortal foods. "Roast beef, I suppose."

"Good choice." He reached one container closer to her, plopping the other one in front of himself, then pulled some paper napkins from the basket. He finished by opening a container filled only with pickles then waited, as usual, for her to begin eating first. "So, if you could do anything, what would it be?" he asked soon after.

She swallowed hastily. "Right now?"

"Well, I'm assuming being a waitress wasn't a dream of yours. What is?"

"I couldn't say." Her role was to support the dreams of others.

His eyebrows twisted quizzically. "Why not?"

"I haven't had a chance to consider."

"What do you mean? You never had a dream? What did you want to be when you were little?"

Her shoulders lifted and dropped, mimicking a motion she had seen at the diner when people had no response to give. Muses were never "little" in the way of human children.

"Well, okay, think about it now. I know you love books. Would you want to write?"

"Oh, no. I love seeing others' stories unfold, but I don't have the imagination necessary to weave compelling ones of my own."

Brett nodded, thinking. "Painting? Or sculpting?"

Allie glanced at her hands. The closest to delicate work they had ever done was braiding her hair. "I don't think so." She should shift the topic to something else.

"Dance? Or music?" he prodded, not giving her a chance.

She shook her head. "Those require talent and years of training."

His shoulders copied her earlier motion. "You seem so passionate for the arts, though. You don't want to try it yourself?"

"Not everyone is destined to be an artist."

"Sure, okay. But most people have dreams, or did at some point."

Allie looked away from his well-intentioned scrutiny. What was the point in having dreams or goals? If she returned to her realm, she would resume guiding others. *When.* Muses weren't allowed hopes and dreams of their own. She glanced back at her former charge. "How do you find a dream?"

Brett finished chewing before answering. "I guess, you try a lot of things, learn about what it's like to do them. And one day, you find something that makes your heart sing."

"Like this," she murmured, looking at the mountains.

"I'd say you could be a florist, but you'd probably hate killing so many flowers."

"I think that would make my heart sob, not sing."

"Well, you could try a little bit of anything that interests you." Encouragement slanted across his expression. "It's never too late to find a dream."

They polished off most of the fruit Brett had brought as he read. Allie had collected the empty glassware, replacing it in the picnic basket, then stretched out beside him, propped on her elbows. Truth be told, he was having a hard time focusing on the pages before him. Even Zafon's masterful words couldn't compete with Alexandra. Unfortunately, he couldn't both gather her close and read the text out here. As if sensing his thoughts, her head dropped back so she could look at him.

Brett let the book close.

"Do you want a break?" she asked from the somewhat bizarre angle.

"Nah. Just thought of something else we could do." Most women would have suspected something inappropriate. Allie just waited for him to continue. "Lie down."

She didn't move until he'd set aside the book and stretched out beside her. Finally, she brushed most of her hair out of the way and dropped her torso to the ground. "What are we doing?"

"Look." He pointed. "There's a seahorse."

Allie's head twisted to shoot him a skeptical look. Brett took her hand and lifted, pointing with their hands together. "See, there's the head, and the little hump, going down into the tail."

"Wow." She laughed lightly. "It's really there."

"What do you see?" He let their hands drop but didn't let go.

"White puffs?"

"No, come on. What do you see?"

He waited as she searched, letting the calm of their surroundings seep into him

"A mermaid," she exclaimed after a while. She gestured with her free hand, outlining the flowing hair and fish tail.

There weren't many other clouds, but they lay there peacefully, side by side, watching the wisps float by.

Allie slipped a tiny spoonful of gelato in her mouth as she considered Brett's question. "Effervescent."

"Oh, that's a good one." They sat on a bench at one edge of the biggest street in his town as locals milled around them. "What about mellifluous?"

She tilted her head disapprovingly, almost like a schoolteacher. "You can do better."

"Surreptitious." That suited a mystery writer.

"Really?" she asked curiously. "That's one of your favorite words?"

Brett busied himself with the stracciatella he held. "Diaphanous."

"Pretty," she acknowledged.

Her approval was oddly satisfying. "Your turn."

"Palimpsest," she answered without hesitation.

Impressive. "Are you sure you don't want to be a writer?"

A breathy laugh escaped her. "I think I'll leave it to you. Your turn."

The setting sun glinted over her hair in a play of colors. "Incandescent," he said softly.

Her laughter slipped into a shy smile.

Brett cleared his throat. "How's the gelato?"

"Delectable," she murmured.

He should be grateful she hadn't gotten a cone. He dipped his spoon in the melting mass he held. "So, what do you say we—"

Wetness splashed his chest, and Allie yelped.

"Sucker!" A punk on a skateboard called rolling away. He high-fived another kid at the end of the block.

Well shit. "Are you all right?"

Obviously stunned, Allie opened her mouth to answer then stopped, looking down at her skirt. A streak of splotches darkened the gray fabric, slanting across her lap and directly over her gelato.

"I'm sorry. I think it's just water. Here, let me get that." He took the paper cup from her hands and stood to dump both in the nearest trashcan.

Allie stood as well.

"I'm sorry." He should say something else.

"Stop, please. It's all right." Her lips twisted to the side. "I cannot say that was something I was expecting, but I'm unharmed. Today has been wonderful. Thank you."

Brett stepped closer, lacing their fingers together. "Yeah? You had a good time?"

Her brows tilted as her eyes narrowed. "It could have been perfect, but—"

He quieted her with a kiss. She had a wholly different smile when he pulled away.

Chapter 14

Allie slipped her clothes off, dropping them onto the soft bench beside the window. Her skirt had mostly dried in the car, but marks from the liquid remained. Did that mean it was destroyed?

More importantly, had this interfered with part of Brett's plan? It wasn't clear what exactly that had been, though their day had been unexpectedly enjoyable until the point when they had been splashed. It had been filled with a relaxed intimacy, with casual touches and pleasant chatter. His focus had been almost exclusively on her, or demonstrating something to her.

As she crossed to the bed, Allie caught her reflection in the mirror that rested above a chest of drawers. The black lingerie she wore featured dark-green curls twining at the edges. Though the coloring made her skin appear even paler, it somehow made her look almost pretty. Brett hadn't even seen it. Wasn't clothless physicality the natural progression to their pleasing encounters?

She was starting to like being seen.

Disregarding any rationality lingering at the edges of her mind, she left the bedroom. The door to Brett's office wasn't fully closed. *The last thing I want is to stop*, he'd claimed the previous night. A relentless whirling of partially imagined continuations and persistently resurfacing memories had plagued her late into the night. She pushed the door open.

Brett looked up from his spot on the couch. His lips parted wordlessly as his eyes trailed over her. His gaze burned into her. Allie swallowed. Had the mortal realm addled her brain?

"Allie…" He really saw her, and he wasn't turning away.

"What if we didn't stop this time?" *Turn around. Walk away, before he throws you out.*

Brett rose from the couch, dropping the shirt he held. He stopped in front of her, slightly out of reach. "Are you sure?"

She smiled, partially in relief, and he seemed to accept that as an answer.

Brett briefly wondered if he had fallen asleep before bending to kiss the spot between Allie's breasts. Faced with the exquisite paleness of her skin, underscored by the black lingerie and the unrestrained curtain of her red hair, he couldn't think. His mouth brushed butterfly kisses down her stomach as his body sank until he knelt before her, almost in worship. Her hands came to rest gently on his shoulders. He exhaled against her skin, and she shivered. In one motion, he hooked one arm behind her knees and stood, catching her upper body with his other arm.

She gasped but soon relaxed into his hold. Her skin slid against his torso. He crossed from his office to his bedroom in record time. On the bed, he lowered her beside him, leaving her legs over his. He slipped his arm from below her knees, using it to brush her hair behind her ear. She watched him with slightly parted lips but didn't move. *She's never done this.*

He kissed her gently. Her mouth opened, and her tongue flicked out against his lips. Groaning, he deepened the kiss. She was a fast learner.

Hating himself, he pulled back just a breath. "Allie."

She hummed in response.

His jaw clenched, as he struggled to breathe. "Are you sure you want to do this?"

Her eyes drifted lower. He closed his and dropped his hand, bracing himself for her answer. Jumping into a frozen river wouldn't be enough to cool him off at this point.

Lips pressed against his jaw. His eyes snapped open. Her mouth brushed tenderly down the side of his neck. Her hair caressed his arm and slid against his chest as he breathed. He snaked his hand through the silken strands to cup her head, pulling her back gently so he could recapture her lips.

Impatient, he flicked her bra open and slipped the straps down her arms. Allie arched against him before drawing back with subtly hunched shoulders. Her hair flowed over and around her torso, hiding her from view in a manner reminiscent of a bashful mermaid. He flung the bra away, freeing her arms, then stood to strip off the jeans that had long ago grown torturously tight.

She scooted away from the edge of the bed, watching him shyly. One arm crossed over her full breasts. Despite the tension vibrating through him, Brett smiled. Gorgeous, clever, innocently beguiling… And tonight, she was all his.

No master could do this justice. Brett stood nearly nude before her, his bronzed body chiseled as though by the hand of an artist, and yet so thoroughly alive in a way no stone, metal, or paint could possibly convey. No wonder she hadn't previously understood.

He settled beside her, legs pressing against hers. Her hair rubbed against and over her as she breathed, unexpectedly teasing her already sensitized skin. Brett's hand directed her chin toward him, and he kissed her unbearably gently. She yearned for more. Allie arched into the kiss, parting her lips as he had so recently taught her. Brett's tongue thrust into her mouth, and his hand moved lower, skimming over her breast. He swallowed her gasp, settling his hand on her rib as he pressed her into the bed.

He balanced above her, mouth skimming down her neck, below her collar, to the inside edges of her breasts. Unthinking, she brushed one hand through the softly resilient mass of his hair. His thumb flicked over her nipple, and her hand dropped, pressing into his shoulder as her torso arced momentarily away from the bed. His chuckle vibrated through her.

Before she could react to the gentle laughter, his tongue joined his lips on her skin. He traced patterns on the mounds of her breasts, thrilling her though somehow her body demanded still more, aching to feel his mouth on an undefined elsewhere. Reading her mind, his lips closed over the peak of one breast. Her breath caught, and she stilled, until he sucked gently, drawing a hum from her throat and curling her fingers in both his muscles and the bed.

His fingers replaced his mouth as it shifted to her other breast. Her body writhed of its own accord, seeking more. When her head pressed into the bed, he moved lower, lips and tongue dancing over her stomach until they found her hip. Barely pausing, he pulled the panties down her legs, abandoning them around her feet to return his attention higher. She kicked them off, unquestioningly. Each touch blended ice and fire in her skin, beckoning even as it burned.

His mouth slowed, licking in longer strokes over one hip as his hand splayed over the other. Her legs rubbed against each other as he continued his onslaught, moving lower to her thigh. His breath blew over the wetness left by his tongue. His fingers trailed the surface of her skin, up and down in an endless, teasing motion.

The gentle pause allowed her to catch her breath even as it sent tremors through her. She looked down her body to him, seeing him see her as her lungs labored. His fingers slipped between her thighs, and his tongue caressed the crevice of her hip as his gaze held hers. Advancing and retreating, his fingers continued to play between her legs until they parted slightly of their own accord. His hand encouraged the separation and moved higher.

Weakened by the overwhelming sensation, her torso dropped. Brett's fingers moved systematically, mimicking the rhythm of his mouth as it tormented the surprisingly sensitive skin of her inner thighs. Warmth and pressure flowed from his masterful manipulation, until his mouth tasted her body where his fingers had played, a place few artists dared to recreate. Her hips arched into the motion. His groans throbbed through her, and sounds accompanied her soft exhalations. The onslaught stopped, and a cry tore from her throat at the loss.

Brett's chuckle accompanied the barest brushing of his lips back over her hips and at the base of her belly, as his fingers slid over her. One plunged inside as the others continued teasing, but she was too swept away by the sensations to be startled. Endless waves crashed over and into her as her body writhed and shivered, manipulated by his hands, and lips, and tongue. When his mouth rejoined his fingers, licking as they moved within her, everything stilled in an unparalleled instant of clarity, before ripples of ecstasy swelled and spread through her.

When her hips ceased the dance he'd directed, Brett spread alongside her, encircling her in his arms. Each touch sent echoes of the pleasure through her, assuring her it hadn't been imagined.

His lips brushed her temple. Her breathing slowed.

The cloth of the undergarment he hadn't discarded scratched her skin, irking her. She twisted in his arms, reaching for the band encircling his hips.

She traced the fabric with her fingers, dipping below it. Should she remove the garment as he had hers? His body, thicker and more solid than the stone of any but the most ancient sculptures, strained against the cloth, pressing against her leg. She wanted the garment gone. Brett watched her intensely but didn't move.

Contemplating her options, she dipped her head to taste his skin, mimicking the outset of his assault on her senses. Brett's fingers tangled in her hair, seeking her back through the loose mass. Her lips traced his warm and firmly pliant muscles. Slight saltiness overlaid the taste she remembered from his neck. She focused on the movement of her mouth, tasting and licking, and her hand dropped, accidently brushing over him. Small motions shivered through his body, and he pulled away.

The last remnant of cloth disappeared, and Allie's eyes explored the revealed flesh. Timidly, she touched this priapic part of him, brushing her fingertips over the heated paradox of soft and hard. Brett hissed, and she snatched her hand back.

"Sorry. Did I hurt you?"

The intensity in his eyes dampened with a flicker of humor. "No." He took her hand in his, guiding it back, letting go when her fingers wrapped loosely around. His eyelids drooped. She brushed her thumb over his tip, and his hand clenched at his side. She skimmed her fingers up his length, grazing him lightly with her nails. A deep groan escaped him.

This. Was. Hell.

Brett strained every muscle to allow Allie the chance to explore to her satisfaction. Her fingers teased with a merciless timidity. He clenched the softness of her hair as the gentle, surface touch tortured him. Her head dipped to his chest, and her fingers wrapped around him once more, squeezing lightly.

He wouldn't last if she kept this up. Forcing his breath out between his teeth, he circled her wrist, drawing her hand away. Confusion curved her brows as she looked up at him.

Swearing under his breath, he reached behind him to the nightstand, ripping open the withdrawn foil packet as she watched, reddened lips beckoning.

Prepared and unable to prolong the wait, he rolled them, angling his body over hers. Her legs separated, welcoming him instinctively. Heat overwhelmed the questioning, and he fed the flames, lowering to kiss her.

Wordlessly, he moved her leg until it wrapped around his hips. Hers bucked, tormenting him further. Seamlessly following his lead, she wrapped her other leg around him. Desperately maintaining his thin hold on his control, he pressed into her slowly. She arched swiftly to meet him and gasped, brows drawing together in a shocked hint of pain.

Brett stilled, bringing his hand to play over her breasts to distract her as her body accepted the stretch. Eventually, her arms came to his ribs then shifted over his back, trailing down and up until her hands pulled his mouth to hers. Her hips shifted beneath him, seeking a rhythm that matched the twining of their tongues. Brett moved in continuous, deep strokes until she writhed beneath his body. She moaned into his mouth as her muscles contracted around him, pulling him with her over the edge.

Allie awoke ensconced in gentle warmth. She stretched slightly, feeling a weight over her waist, their legs wound together, and a growing pressure behind her thigh. Brett hummed a low note. His lips found her ear.

"Stop wiggling," he murmured.

She emptied her lungs, relaxing into his hold. His hand moved up her ribs to cup her breast. She twisted partially to him, but his mouth on her jaw blocked the movement. His fingers teased her nipple, rekindling the flames he had stoked the night before. She shifted toward his hand and arched her hips into him. The pressure grew harder. His teeth bit her earlobe softly.

His hand dropped from her breast as he resettled behind her, shifting her hair from between their bodies. His mouth moved to her neck and trailed down her spine as his fingers fluttered over her stomach and chest.

Allie let her eyes drift shut, luxuriating in the shifting pinpoints of pleasure. Brett continued lower, disentangling their legs. When he reached the sensitive center of her lower back, she gasped. His tongue traced loops on her skin. Fully roused from sleep, she bent her legs, sliding down the bed, then twisted to face him.

His lips curled. "G'morning."

Chapter 15

Brett whistled as he made breakfast. Well, brunch, technically. He sure didn't mind waking up to Allie in his arms, and no man in his right mind would complain about what had followed.

He pulled the eggs from the fridge when the main bathroom's shower shut off. He'd considered suggesting they shower together but didn't want to wear her out. So he'd grabbed his stuff and ceded the master bath to her.

Allie joined him just as he was sliding the stuffed French toast into the oven. She'd somehow managed to secure her wet hair up and completely out of the way. He couldn't help being disappointed, though it was understandably practical. "You got dressed."

Her cheeks flushed with a light trace of color. She was almost shyer when they were both properly covered. "As did you."

"Yeah, well." He walked over to her spot at the edge of the island and smiled. "You're prettier to look at than I am."

A matching smile lit her features. "I feel obliged to disagree."

Brett couldn't resist cupping her face and stealing a kiss. He pulled back with a final brush of the lips. "Do you have to work today?"

She hummed in the affirmative. "At two."

"Do you want a ride?"

"I don't mind walking."

He let her go reluctantly to pour her the juice with which she started every morning. "You're starting later than usual."

"Yes. It will also be my first time spending the majority of my shift on my own. Thankfully, Hal promised he would be there to lock up."

"Lock up? You're closing tonight?" He didn't like the thought of her alone at the diner so late at night.

"Thank you," she murmured, accepting the juice. "Hal will technically be closing the doors."

"When's your shift over?"

"Ten." She put down her glass and moved efficiently around the kitchen, setting the table for them. It was absurdly homey. "Or perhaps ten thirty. Wanda mentioned that it may be extended due to unforeseeable circumstances."

"I'll come pick you up then."

"You don't have to do that. Particularly since I can't be certain when I would be finished."

"It's not all that safe for you to walk alone at night." Not that it was an unsafe neighborhood, but there was no point taking chances. She looked at him as though the concept was wholly foreign. "There's a very low chance that anything bad would happen, but I just don't think we should risk it."

Her lips flattened into each other. "Whatever you say."

Brett pulled her closer using her jeans' belt loops. The proximity she'd welcomed minutes ago seemed to startle her. "What's wrong?"

"I would prefer not to inconvenience you." She broke eye contact, adding, "Any more than I already have."

She'd assimilated into his life so effortlessly, he'd almost forgotten how unusual their situation actually was. "It isn't an inconvenience. Really. It's good for me to get out of the house at least once in a while. Pretend I'm part of the real world." Skepticism still tinged her expression. "Besides, I thought you were going to work on that whole distressed damsel thing."

A few heartbeats later, her chuckle mingled with the oven timer. Brett dropped a kiss on her lips before stepping away.

Allie paused after leaving the diner's kitchen, allowing the door to swing shut behind her. Brett leaned on the bar, tapping a rhythm with his fingers. Thus far, she had successfully avoided contemplating the night before. Or that morning. Seeing him now, she wanted nothing more than to curl into his arms, despite the confusion raging within her. She shook her head at the ridiculous desire and strode through the empty diner.

Brett flashed her a relaxed smile. "You all set?"

His hand settled on her back as they walked to the car. Allie handed him the envelope she held before they sat down.

"What's this?"

"Payment, for my first week." Seven days. Infinitely longer than she had once thought she would ever spend in mortal form. She had, however, proven Kristie's unfavorable expectations to be incorrect. "Hal said he would continue employing me. So, I can begin repaying you."

His expression was inscrutable in the darkened lot. "You sure that's what you want?"

"Certainly. That was the intention." Being financially indebted to him was even less desirable after the physical intimacy they had shared.

"All right, but you should keep at least some. Have some cash on hand."

Allie couldn't imagine what she may need to purchase, but it didn't seem worth arguing. "If you say so."

He opened the car door for her, ending the uncomfortable topic. She slid in silently.

"So how was your shift?" he asked, turning on the car.

"Fairly quiet. Nate stopped by, the artist, who—"

"Yeah, I know who you mean."

"He invited us to a small showing he is having, on Friday."

"Oh?" It was impossible to gauge the mood behind the syllable, though of course he was concentrating on maneuvering the car.

"He said it would mostly be pieces he has been working on lately. I don't actually know whether you enjoy paintings?"

"Well, I'm a fan of the one painting of his I've seen."

"You've seen his work?" She hadn't considered it, but it wasn't entirely surprising that the two had previously crossed paths.

He stopped the car in the garage and looked at her, eyebrows drawing up over humor-filled eyes. Comprehension warmed her cheeks, and she turned away, unable to maintain eye contact. The sultry knowledge in that painting was a far cry from Allie's limited experience, even after the night before.

Brett didn't bother hiding his smile. She was so adorable sometimes. He stopped in front of the door to the main house, and Allie tilted her head to look up at him. Only a few wisps had escaped her strict hairstyle. Brett stuffed his hands in his pockets to prevent himself from disheveling her further. "Are you tired?"

"Did you have something in mind?"

So many somethings. Standing in the garage wasn't one of them, so he opened the door and waited for her to enter the house. "We could play cards. Or read, or something. Unless you want to go straight to bed?" *Shit.* "To sleep." *Smooth.* Then again, there weren't exactly guidelines for this situation in Emily Post handbooks. Or there might be, it wasn't like he'd read any.

"I would be happy to stay awake, but you aren't required to entertain me, by any means. Especially if you need to work."

He hadn't considered the possibility that she wouldn't want to spend the night with him again. "Would you like me to… Did you want to be alone tonight?"

Her lips parted and pressed together several times before she finally answered. "Preferably not, but I wouldn't want—"

"To be an inconvenience," he finished for her.

"Precisely."

"Allie." He brushed a stray wisp back and tugged gently on her earlobe, before brushing his thumb over her jaw. "You're incredibly beautiful, and funny, and smart, when you're not holding yourself back. The last thing being with you is is an inconvenience." In fact, he should maybe be thanking whatever had plopped her down in his office.

The stunning green of her irises disappeared behind her eyelids for a prolonged moment. When she finally looked back at him, the uncertainty in her eyes winded him. He dropped a kiss on her lips. If she didn't believe him, he'd just have to convince her. "Your feet must be killing you."

The shift in topic seemed to draw her back to solid ground. "Somewhat," she admitted.

"Well, then." He bowed slightly, gesturing deeper into the house with one arm and feeling like a complete idiot until she offered him a small smile as she passed. "What would you like to do?"

"Whatever you would like." *Well that's entirely too tempting.* She glanced back at him. "Would you mind if I changed?"

"Not at all." Though he had to bite back some suggestions.

"So, did you decide if you want to play cards? Or read?" Brett asked as Allie settled beside him on the couch.

Her hair fanned out, and her knees folded onto the cushion. "What would we read?"

"Whatever you'd like."

"What about something you're working on?"

Brett bristled at the question. It wasn't all that strange that she'd be curious about his writing, but he didn't share his works in progress. And he definitely couldn't show her this one. "How about something else?"

Her teeth closed over her bottom lip.

Brett reached for her hand and wound their fingers together. "I just really abhor showing my work to anyone before it's ready."

Her lip slipped out, but she didn't comment. He drew circles in her palm with his thumb as she watched him.

"'Abhor' is a good word," she finally murmured.

"It sums up my loathing and reluctance pretty well." Her head ducked, but at least she didn't let go of his hand. Brett squeezed her fingers lightly. "It's not a reflection on you, or how I think about you."

She nodded, eyes still trained on her lap. "All right."

More relieved than he should have been, he brought her hand up to kiss the center of her palm. Her eyes met his, and he let their hands drift lower, shifting closer to kiss her. Their lips slipped together almost chastely, tempting him with so much more. Maybe he could teach her strip poker.

After beating Brett in another heated game of "Egyptian Ratscrew"—which had absolutely nothing to do with Egypt, or rats—Allie rose to stretch. "I'm going to go get a glass of water. Would you like something?"

"Just my pride back," he teased with the smile she found endlessly appealing.

Thoughts jumbled around in her head as she moved through his home, attempting to sort through the compliments he had paid her earlier, his reluctance to share his work, the physical passion they had shared, and her own chaotic feelings about this situation and her previously reluctant host. She should have been seeking that loophole in the spell, but she hadn't pursued the question of her transformation as effectively as was necessary. The idea of remaining in this realm, of living out her limited mortal days like this, with Brett, was no longer thoroughly repulsive, but could she turn her back on her true form? Moreover, was there any reason to believe his interest in her was more than simply transient?

The only times the questions stilled were when she was thoroughly distracted by the diner's patrons or when Brett touched her. Or smiled at her. Like he was currently doing from his seat on the couch. He held his hand out, and she set her glass on the low table before him to take it. He pulled her forward until she stood beside him then tugged sharply so she fell into his lap. Instantly, his arms circled her.

A low laugh escaped her, only to fade away. Sitting like this, there was no evading his gaze. Her hands came to the front of his shoulders. She wanted the closeness of their bodies entwined.

Brett's hands moved to her sides, over her ribs, and around to her back, softly stroking. Humor had been replaced by intensity. Nothing but a need she couldn't define remained.

Her hands dropped to the hem of his shirt, hating in that moment the conventions of human propriety that kept the material between them. Brett mimicked the motion, sliding his hands under her top. They leaned together into a kiss, lips and tongues teasing and tangling, leaving both of them breathless. Brett didn't move, waiting for some hidden key or command. It didn't seem like he would object to a repeat of the previous night, and yet, though he didn't ask this time, he was still allowing her the choice.

Allie slid from his lap, standing to remove her top. Despite the preceding night, she fought not to shield herself from his eyes as they stilled on her torso. She clutched the material in her fist before flinging it away with deceptive confidence as her lungs stilled, awaiting his response while her heart pounded on.

Brett shifted forward on the couch, bringing his hands to her bared waist. He pressed a kiss to the top of her abdomen, and her breath blew out as her muscles clenched. Unrelenting, his tongue traced patterns she couldn't follow over her skin. Her hair fell over both of them as her head bent, and her hands dropped to his shoulders. Brett's fingers flexed softly into her then moved to the front of her jeans, barely hesitating before undoing the fastenings. His mouth paused in tasting her as he glanced up, catching her gaze. Allie raised onto her toes so the irritating material lowered in his hands. He stripped the offending fabric away, bending to kiss lower on her belly.

Allie pressed him back, yearning to touch his skin as he felt hers. She knelt on the couch, settling over his lap so she could focus on lifting his shirt. Brett gripped her hips for an instant before helping her expose his torso. As their lips met once more, his hands searched through her hair, seeking the back of her bra. His fingers fumbled with the material before Allie realized the problem.

"Front," she murmured, attempting to break the kiss so she could explain, but Brett recaptured her lips, now effortlessly finding and unhooking the clasp. Shoving the material aside, his hands cupped her breasts, thumbs flicking over her nipples. Her hips ground into his lap, and he moaned into her mouth. He slipped the straps down her arms, and she let the fabric fall.

Brett brushed her hair to the sides, so it framed her breasts rather than shielding them. His hands splayed over her ribs as he bent to tease her with his mouth. Allie lifted off his lap, arching toward him. His teeth grazed her nipple, and she didn't fight the moan it drew from her. His arms slipped between her legs to deal with his own jeans, stray touches tantalizing her as his mouth continued nibbling.

When he pulled back, air prickled along her moistened skin. Her hips dropped of their own accord, closer to his lap. He cradled her back in one hand as he flipped them, lowering her onto the couch. She wriggled against him, adjusting her position, and he nearly growled before fully kicking off the jeans.

He pressed between her legs, and Allie rose to meet his lips, running her hands over his burning torso. His hips shifted rhythmically, and he swallowed the sounds it drew from her throat despite the interfering fabric. Nothing mattered other than the man above her.

Brett tore himself away from Allie, sitting back on his heels. Her legs were still loosely wrapped, low around his. They couldn't keep going without protection, but getting up was out of the question. She watched him from beneath lowered lids, arching into his hands that lay on her ribs, feeling her lungs expand. He slid his fingers up over her breasts, and she writhed against him, challenging his self-control.

He moved back on the couch, tracing her curves until he reached the scrap of fabric still covering her, marring the flawless lines of her luminous skin. Allie shifted with his hands. He slipped two fingers under the strings holding her panties together and lowered them over her legs, moving further back himself.

Her thigh cushioned his cheek as he blew across her. She shivered, and he hummed as he tasted her. He licked and kissed and sucked gently until her hips undulated, seeking his attentions. He shifted to her inner thigh, loving her slightly frustrated moan as he focused on the sensitive skin at the juncture of her hips. Her hand brushed through his hair, and he willingly moved back where she wanted him.

She breathed his name, and he sent her flying.

Once Allie's body stilled, she sat up, moving to his end of the couch. She straddled him again, bracing her hands on his chest, and a small tremor ran through her. Her hair floated against his arms, and he brushed it back, running his fingers through the strands. Her head dipped to his chest, lips brushing gently over his skin, drawing pinpoints of pleasure. She traced lower, and he froze, flexing his fingers in her hair.

"Allie." She gazed up along the length of his body without moving, eyes glinting with mischief and an innate knowledge. "You don't have to—"

She ignored him, refocusing on trailing her mouth down his stomach. She slid to the floor, slipping her fingers under the elastic of his underwear, and he lifted off the couch so she could free him. Her fingers wrapped around him, and his head fell back. She squeezed gently, and his hand brushed softly over her face. The thought that she shouldn't be on the floor flashed through his mind, but her tongue flicked out, tasting his tip. Her lips brushed him gently as her fingers stroked, and all thought disappeared.

Her hair teased his legs as she explored, swirling her tongue over him before taking him into her mouth. Her fingers mimicked his earlier movements, brushing over his hips and thighs as she sucked gently, nearly bringing him off the couch.

Her tongue danced delicately over him, driving him to madness. Her breath puffed over him when she glanced up with a flash of uncertainty. His knuckles skimmed her cheek, feeling the muscles shift as her lips curled. With newfound confidence, she tasted him, teasing and tormenting until the swell of sensation swept through him.

Chapter 16

Damn if he wasn't the luckiest man alive. Sunlight was streaming into the bedroom, and birds literally chirped outside the window. Brett fingered the red coil on his stomach, careful not to wake Allie. The passion on the couch had been only the beginning of their night, which had progressed into the bedroom long before they had gotten to sleep.

Being with her was nothing like he had imagined, and written. Whereas his character was a mysterious but assertive vixen, innocence that couldn't be faked tinged Allie's every move. She was artless, wholly incapable of the guile he had at first suspected. Incomparable.

As though feeling the weight of his thoughts, Allie shifted, sighing. Her eyes opened partially, revealing the piercing green, then shut, almost in a reverse blink. A soft curve pulled at her lips as her eyes drifted open once more.

"G'morning," Brett murmured.

She stretched against him, humming, and Brett raised onto one elbow to brush her lips.

"Hi," she breathed. Little crinkles accented the easy joy in her eyes.

"You hungry? Used up a lot of energy last night."

She chuckled breathlessly, blushing, and broke eye contact. Brett smiled at the play of color that accompanied her shyness. She sobered when her gaze returned to him, and he leaned down for another soft kiss. "So?"

"I think I would prefer a shower, if you wouldn't object."

Brett drew away reluctantly, sitting up. They couldn't literally spend the whole day in bed. "You could take a bubble bath. Relax."

"A bubble bath?" Allie propped herself up onto her elbows. The sheet that covered her slipped down, revealing not quite enough and tempting him to test his earlier stance. He got up to pull on some sweatpants instead.

"I think you'll like it," he said, surveying the enticement on the bed. "I can draw one for you. You can soak, unwind." Her mouth opened. "And don't say anything about inconveniencing me." Her lips twisted to the side. Brett leaned over her, arms sinking slightly into the mattress.

Allie's chin tilted toward him, inviting his kiss. He kept it light, brushing her lips with his in a soft sequence.

"What will you do?" she asked, when he lifted away.

"Might go for a run."

"Why?"

He smiled despite himself. "Not all of us can be as effortlessly sexy as you, and I've been slacking off lately. Since before I met you," he added, preventing her protests before dragging himself away.

Allie brushed her hair languidly in front of the fogged-over mirror. The bath Brett had filled for her had been soothing, warmth seeping into every muscle as a soft fragrance floated around her, entirely altering the experience. Even the persistent ache in her feet had washed away. She twisted her hair in a coil, securing the end with her clip almost thoughtlessly. Incredible how recently she had been flabbergasted by such simple actions.

Heated memories flooded her as she entered the bedroom. Spending the remainder of the day with Brett was a tantalizing proposition. Each time they came together spun passionate caresses into unparalleled pleasure, complemented by the progressing comfort of their association. At times, she was swept away by the newfound ease of her situation, as though it could continue indefinitely. Which, sensibly, it could not. Allie still had to unravel whatever spell had been cast, though she refused to consider the ramifications of her success.

She dropped the towel onto the bed and selected a matching bra-and-pantie set, fashioned from a vaguely floral lace overlaid on a sheer, lightly tan fabric.

Brett's keys jangled as he returned from running, and Allie smiled, envisioning his reaction to her choice. She slipped on a soft tee shirt and went to meet him. Three shrill tones led her to the kitchen.

"Woah." A young woman's eyes scanned Allie's scantily clad body.

Allie fisted her hands in the hem of her top and pulled it down as surreptitiously as possible. How could she have forgotten the clothing he had given her when she had first materialized? It wasn't unreasonable to assume this was their owner.

The woman brought one hand onto a cocked hip. "Guess Brett wasn't expecting me."

Allie returned her regard, stalled in the entrance to the kitchen and unable to formulate a greeting or explanation. The woman wore a black tee shirt and paint-splattered pants. Her brown hair featured hints of pink. She was undoubtedly human, and yet her lithe form more closely approximated that of many muses than Allie's own.

"So where is he?" she asked.

"He went running."

"And he left you behind?"

Allie couldn't formulate a response. Had she truly been so immeasurably wrong in her assessment of their developing relationship? Clearly, this woman played an intimate role in his life, unabashedly entering his home and comfortably utilizing the kitchen. Allie was nothing more than an intruder. "I'm sorry."

A whistled melody trailed her apology. Allie turned slightly to see Brett stroll into the house. He flashed her a bright smile and came to wrap his arms around her. The woman cleared her throat. Brett dropped his arms and stiffened.

"Vicky! Why didn't you tell me you were coming home early? I would have come pick you up."

"Jess gave me a ride. And I'm actually going by Vic now."

"I could switch to Victoria."

The woman scrunched her nose. Allie enjoyed the brief moment of invisibility. Perhaps being unseen wasn't as terrible as she had once believed.

"So you've been busy," Victoria said.

"Vicky!" Brett snapped, shooting the woman a look Allie couldn't understand. The woman smirked and raised one eyebrow. "Vicky, this is Allie—Alexandra." He placed one hand on Allie's back. "Allie, this is Vicky."

"Vic," the woman corrected.

"My sister," Brett finished.

Allie glanced between them while the words registered. "Your…" Her mind finally caught up. "It's nice to meet you," she redirected lamely.

Victoria's eyes narrowed. "Jury's still out."

"Vicky!"

"What?" She shrugged.

"I'm sorry." Brett's thumb moved gently on Allie's back. "She must have forgotten her manners back in Paris."

"Sorry my coming home is interrupting your fun," his sister grumbled.

"Oh I'm sure you being back will be plenty of fun," Brett said drily.

Victoria didn't answer, looking away from both of them.

"Hey." The syllable snapped her gaze back to Brett. "It's good to have you home. I'm even glad Paris didn't destroy that smart-aleck mouth of yours."

Victoria's features resettled into a small, hesitant smile. "Someone's gotta keep you on your toes." She shifted her attention to Allie, and the trace of humor disappeared. "Or, is that what you're for?"

"Vicky, I swear to—"

"Okay, okay." Perplexingly, they smiled at each other.

Before this moment, Allie would have claimed she had become more adept at understanding the peculiarities of human interactions in her time among mortals, but the siblings had wholly thrown her. She retreated to familiar territory. "You are a painter," she ventured into the silence.

Both heads turned to her. "Not exclusively," Victoria acknowledged.

"Vicky just spent a semester studying art in Paris."

"That must have been an extraordinary experience for you. The range and quality of work displayed in the city, not to mention the creative history..." Allie trailed off when Brett's hand dropped.

"Oh, you've been?" Victoria asked, less antagonistically, though perhaps that was wishful thinking.

"Paris has quite a reputation."

A blasting tone outside broke the resulting silence.

"Well, I for one am looking forward to hearing all about your semester," Brett said. "Are you hungry? I can whip something up for us."

The tone repeated, sounding three times. "Don't kill me," Victoria said, brushing past them and out of the kitchen, "but I actually have plans with Jess for the afternoon."

Brett followed, but Allie didn't move, affording them some semblance of privacy though she could hear the conversation clearly enough.

"It's your first day back," Brett said. "Or were you not even planning on telling me you'd returned."

"I thought you'd be working! You know if I stay home, I'll end up taking a nap, and then there's that whole jet lag thing. Besides, it looks like you're in good hands."

"All right, that's it. Get out." Allie couldn't help smiling at his teasing tone. The siblings obviously had an affectionate, if confounding, relationship. "Back for dinner?"

"You bet."

When the door closed, Allie crossed the hallway to the bedroom to change. Clearly, forgoing bottoms had been a horrendous idea.

Brett turned from the door to see Allie disappear into the bedroom. She had wholly closed off in the kitchen. Apparently she had an impenetrable poker face. Granted, Vicky was always tough on newcomers.

He was thrilled Vicky was home, but it was a good thing he'd had the presence of mind to toss the clothes they'd discarded last night into the office before his run. He hadn't expected to have to introduce them so soon. Still, it could've gone worse. And Vicky hadn't been wrong; he definitely wasn't opposed to spending some more time alone with Allie.

Stifling the resurgence of suspicion that came from his desire to shelter Vicky from any more disappointment, Brett rapped his knuckles on the bedroom door. It swung open from the pressure, revealing Allie seated on the bed. Her lips pressed together, and her hands were clasped in her lap, clutching her black skirt.

Brett leaned against the doorframe. "You all right?" He wouldn't mind getting her back to the mindset that had led her to wearing nothing but a tee shirt.

She forced a smile. "I didn't know you had a sister."

Brett stiffened. Vicky was a nonnegotiable part of his life.

"I wouldn't have…" She trailed off, looking down at the skirt.

His lips twitched as he understood. "You wouldn't have offended her delicate sensibilities by walking around half-naked?" he teased, approaching the bed.

Allie's head tilted back so she could look up at him. One eyebrow dipped over tense eyes. Brett crouched before her, and her gaze followed his movement.

"I think she'll get over it," he said, working the skirt from her grasp. The partial nudity wasn't Vicky's main issue. "I, for one, think you're wearing way too much as it is."

Her gaze flicked to the open doorway. "What about Victoria?"

"Well, for one thing, if you want to score any points with her, call her Vic. For another"—he pressed his arms onto the bed to rise over her—"she won't be back for at least a few hours."

He captured Allie's lips, and she gradually relaxed into the kiss. Her hands came to his ribcage, but Brett pulled away, still sweaty from his run. "I am going to jump in the shower quickly. Don't you dare get dressed." He brushed her lips once more then backed away. Allie watched him from the bed, smiling softly. This was going to be the fastest shower known to man.

Allie lay curled against Brett, drawing patterns on his abs with her finger. He glanced over at the clock and groaned. "I have to go make dinner."

"Right now?"

"It's Vicky's first night home." Plus, they hadn't eaten since breakfast. "She just spent five months eating in Paris. I can't compare with that, but I still want to make it special." His hand trailed over her back.

"You truly care for her."

"Yeah, of course."

"Was she with your parents in Paris?"

Brett's jaw clenched, even though it was a perfectly reasonable question. "Just studying abroad. Our parents aren't in the picture."

"I'm sorry…"

"We did just fine without them." And there was no need to think about them now. "You know what else we should do?"

"Hmm?" Her hand dipped lower, under the sheet.

Brett laughed. "Not quite what I meant."

Her hand stopped. Brett dug his fingers gently into her side. "I was going to say, we should do laundry." He rolled them over. "But I like your idea better."

"Laundry?"

"Well, I'm all right with you walking around naked if you are." He ducked to taste her neck.

Her legs twisted around his. "What about my job?"

"Definitely need clothes for that," he said against her skin. She shivered and arched under him.

"So…we need to do laundry, for our clothes?"

Brett lifted his head to look at her. A light pink in her cheeks brought out the already vibrant green of her eyes. "It can wait."

Chapter 17

So, can I borrow the car?" Vic asked the next morning. Dinner had gone somewhat better than their first encounter, though Allie had still excused herself rather early, allowing the siblings privacy. She had fallen asleep alone, but at least she had awoken in Brett's arms.

"Did you reactivate your U.S. phone?" he asked.

Vic's eyes rolled up to the ceiling before she looked back at her brother. "You worried about me less when I was literally thousands of miles way, in a big bad city."

"No, I didn't. I just couldn't do anything about it, thousands of miles away."

Allie didn't interfere, sipping her orange juice.

"But now you can?"

"Well,"—Brett grinned—"I could not let you take the car."

"You know I'm not actually a child anymore, right? I could even give you a ride to work, if you want," she offered Allie, switching tactics.

"Oh. That's generous of you to suggest, but I don't mind walking." She was certainly not going to interfere with their decisions.

"Or, I could give her a ride. Not a reason for you to take the car." Brett polished off the last of his eggs and smiled.

"I want to swing by Blank Canvas and get some fresh supplies. What happened to being supportive of my art? Besides, I thought you'd like having the house to yourself to work. Don't you have a deadline coming up?"

"All right, all right." His hands flipped up in surrender. "But we need groceries, so you can swing by the store on your way home."

Vic grinned. "Whatever you say. Text me a list?" She downed her remaining juice in one sip, stood, and looked at Allie. "So, we'll leave in like, five?" She strode out of the kitchen without waiting for an answer.

"She doesn't have to drive me," Allie protested, though she knew it was futile.

"Scared of being alone with her?" he teased.

"I am fairly certain I can handle her." She did have several hundred years of experience navigating capricious fae personalities. One young mortal could hardly be worse. She twirled her fork in the remnants of food on her plate. "Perhaps she'll even somewhat satiate my curiosity about you."

"Oh, do I not satisfy you?"

Allie's cheeks warmed, though she should have anticipated the retort. Brett rounded the table as she scrambled for a response. He braced his arms on the back of her chair and the corner of the table, leaning over her. Allie twisted to face him. "Your attentions are sufficient." A gross understatement.

Brett smiled, obviously seeing through her feigned composure. "So what is it you want to know about me?"

"Anything worth knowing," she answered without hesitation.

"Let's see. I love my sister."

"I gathered that."

"I write, mostly mystery novels."

She smiled, and he lowered to brush her lips.

"And I think you're fascinating." Another soft brush. "And stunning." A third. "And sexy as hell."

This kiss deepened. Until an exaggerated cough from the corner separated them. Brett stepped back, still smiling, and offered Allie his hand. She stood to follow Vic to the garage.

"Have a good day. And drive safe!" Brett called after them.

Vic hadn't said much during the brief drive to the diner, but since virtually every table was filled, Allie had no time to ponder this new factor to her existence in the mortal realm. For once, Kristie appeared happy to see her. Both of them dashed among the tables, barely pausing until an hour into Allie's shift when the crowd suddenly thinned as though by design.

"I'm gonna take a break," Kristie said, heading for the kitchen.

Allie nodded and started a fresh pot of coffee brewing, then turned to wipe down the miscellany of sticky spots on the bar. Three tables remained: a trio of young travelers studying a worn map, a struggling storyteller scribbling on napkins, and an older couple, who was more interested in each other than the cooling food on their table.

Technically, Allie was older than they were, at least in mortal terms, yet somehow they seemed more experienced, wiser. They held hands and watched each other as though sharing a secret intended only for the two of them. Did mortals have secrets unknown in faerie?

The door clunked shut, distracting her. Nate approached the bar, lips slanted in a half smile. Allie's lips curved of their own volition, until she noticed the brown package in his hands. Surely he wouldn't have brought her another painting, especially while Kristie was working.

"How's it going?" he asked, settling on a stool. He rested the package before him, between his arms, as though sheltering it. Paint splotches still covered his fingers.

"Unexpectedly busy earlier, actually. Can I get you anything?"

"Half-caf, please." She brought out a fresh cup and poured his coffee. "Did you have a good weekend? You seem happier."

"It was…" She paused, searching for an appropriate word. "Unprecedented." What a bland description for a sensational several days. Was she happier? Certainly compared to her first days in the mortal realm. But overall? She couldn't possibly be more content here than in faerie, even if any time she spent with Brett did thoroughly enliven and delight her. "How are you doing?"

"Well, you know. Getting ready for that show Friday. Some people actually said they're coming, so I can't back out now."

"I'm certainly interested in seeing more of your work."

"Thanks." His smile flashed momentarily, and he tapped his fingers erratically on the package. "I was actually hoping, maybe you'd do me a favor?"

"A favor?" The traveling trio gestured for her before Nate had a chance to answer. "I'll return in a moment."

He nodded, and Allie rounded the bar, pondering as she gave this table their check and passed by the others automatically. Would this favor have something to do with his painting, or his show?

Kristie came out of the kitchen but stopped abruptly when she saw Nate. Early lunch customers entered the diner, and she veered to greet and seat them. Nate turned when she spoke, and his customarily nonchalant expression drooped.

Allie waited at his side until he refocused on her. "What can I do for you?" Perhaps the favor he sought would help remove his distress.

"Oh, uh. I was hoping you could give this to Kristie." His fingers brushed the top of the package. "Maybe mention the show? Friday?"

"Of course." Simple enough, if one discounted Kristie's animosity.

"Thanks." His lips tried to pull into a smile, though they didn't quite make it. He withdrew a five-dollar bill from his pocket and placed it beside his nearly untouched coffee. "I should get back to work." He held the door open for a chattering group of women before leaving. Allie tucked the package away, collected menus, and walked over to greet them.

"You wanna help me with the groceries?"

Brett hit save and turned to face Vicky, leaning back in his chair. "Didn't you learn to be self-sufficient in your time abroad?"

"You know, I mostly hung out in the catacombs, drank a lot, participated in some orgies. Not a lot of solo activities."

Brett pushed out of the chair. "You're hilarious."

"What makes you think I'm kidding?" she asked, walking away. "I've never seen bodies painted quite that way," she added by the car.

He absolutely would not take the bait. "Did you get everything?"

"I dunno. I might need a refresher course."

"Vicky!"

"Yes, I got everything in your text. They do have grocery stores in France, you know. " She grabbed a couple bags and stalked past him into the house.

Brett picked up the rest and closed the trunk, then followed her. He set the bags on the island. "You want to talk about it?"

Vicky slammed the cupboard shut and spun around. "You really didn't waste any time, did you?"

"What are you talking about?"

"Alexandra." She exaggerated the pronunciation, drawing out the name.

"I've dated before, Vicky. You should give her a chance."

"She *lives* here. With you. That's not dating. How long after I left did that take?"

"Don't be stupid." Her brows flattened, and her jaw clenched. Brett crossed the few steps to her and took hold of her shoulders. She didn't look at him. "Vicky. I'm not going anywhere. You're my priority, no matter what." He hadn't known she questioned that.

"You're not my legal guardian anymore."

"I'm your brother. You can't get rid of me that easy."

Vicky's jaw shifted from side to side.

Brett looped one arm around her shoulders and led her to the island, pressing her onto a stool. "Where's all this coming from?"

"We both know you haven't had much of a life because of me. You haven't seriously dated in years. Clearly I'm in the way."

"That's the stupidest thing I've ever heard you say. Including the time you wanted to refashion one of gram's dresses as a surprise for her birthday and ended up shredding it." Her lips twitched at the memory. "I love you. And I'm not going any-where. But that doesn't mean I'm going to be single forever." Or at least, he hoped not.

She sighed, finally looking him in the eyes. "I know. I wouldn't want you to. I was just surprised, I guess. You didn't even mention her."

He wasn't about to admit Allie hadn't been around all that long. Was it really just over a week? "I know. I should have. Things moved kind of quickly."

"You really like her."

He didn't comment.

"Is she 'the one'?"

Brett passed his hand over his eyes then through his hair. "I don't know. That's not the point."

"Yeah it is." She shrugged. "I was being a brat. I don't know what I'd do without you."

"You sound like an afterschool special." She rolled her eyes, and Brett smiled.

"She makes you happy?"

"She's incredible."

Vicky slipped off the stool and resumed putting away the groceries. "Just keep the noise down," she added over her shoulder.

"Victoria Jane!"

She spun around and grinned. She didn't know it, but Brett forgave just about anything when she smiled. "You almost got it that time. Just like grandma."

The lunch rush continued in waves until Kristie's shift was almost over. When only the customary artists were left, Allie approached her. "Kristie, may I speak with you a moment?"

The waitress considered her before nodding. "Crazy day today," she commented, following Allie behind the bar. "You handled yourself okay."

The compliment, of sorts, derailed Allie's thoughts a moment. "Thank you," she finally said. "I have something for you." Allie withdrew the brown rectangle and held it out.

Kristie's eyes narrowed as her lips pursed. "I don't really need to see another painting of you."

Allie placed the package beside her on the bar. "I don't know what's inside, but I sincerely doubt it has anything to do with me." When Kristie didn't move, she added, "You should open it." A flash of inspiration hit her, and Allie glanced around briefly for its source before refocusing. "Or I could open it for you."

Kristie snatched the package away. She sighed, then tore open the packaging. Her portrait peeked out—an idealized replica with shining tears highlighting her eyes and soft colors caressing her skin and hair, so she shone. Allie picked up a coffee pot and went to check on the tables, though they weren't in need of her attention. When she returned to replace the pot, Kristie was still staring at the canvas.

"What the hell am I supposed to do with this?" The question was directed more to the canvas than to Allie.

"He's having a small showing on Friday. He asked that you attend."

"Why would he think I'd do that? Because of a stupid painting?" She let the piece in question fall to the bar.

"You don't see it?"

Kristie's gaze flew to her. "He painted me crying, like a sniveling idiot. What, that's supposed to be flattering?"

As if the painting had provided new insight to the waitress' inner world, Allie glimpsed bewilderment behind the hostility.

"He loves you," she answered simply. She may never have felt it herself, but she had seen countless mortals express it in their work. "It's in every brushstroke."

"So, you're an art critic now?"

Allie ignored the barb, sensitive to the vulnerability Nate's painting had exposed—vulnerability Kristie was apparently accustomed to hiding. "Look again. Everything about that painting is his version of a love letter. Sincere beauty and a depth of emotion unparalleled by a smile. He genuinely sees you, and adores what he sees. Not many have that."

Kristie didn't answer for an extended moment, regarding first the painting and then Allie again. "Do you?"

Allie swallowed. "No."

"What about with Brett?"

"He is the closest I have ever come." Though he didn't believe she could exist, nor did he share himself fully with her. Everything they had shared had been nothing more than superficial, and she had to remember that.

"You know," Kristie ventured, truly looking at Allie. "Love isn't the same for everyone. Maybe one type is trusting someone to care about you for who you are now, not because of the damage of your past."

Allie couldn't continue down that uncertain path, particularly while working, despite Kristie's unexpected perceptiveness. This conversation wasn't about the muddled emotions she was struggling to control, nor could she afford for it to be. "Does that mean you'll go to Nate's opening?"

Kristie tapped the edge of the canvas and sighed. "I can't really ignore an invitation like this, can I?"

✧ ✧ ✧

Amazingly, Brett was making pretty good progress on his book. After his talk with Vicky, the troubles of his characters were a welcome distraction. He didn't realize Allie had come home until she knocked on the doorframe. He twisted halfway to see her. "Hey."

"Hi, there."

He glanced at the screen, trying to hold on to elusive bits of dialogue. "How was your day?" The characters kept whispering.

"I should let you work."

He tore his eyes from the screen. Small signs of humor touched her lips and the edges of her eyes. "Sorry. I just need a few minutes."

"I can wait." She stepped away, and Brett twisted back around in his chair to resume typing. He wasn't quite sure where he was going, but he did feel kind of bad for Pete, having his reputation questioned, doubting his own sanity. And things were developing pretty well so far.

Chapter 18

Brett didn't look up again until a few halfway-decent pages later. Vicky was out reconnecting with friends, but Allie was probably around somewhere. He stretched his arms up to the ceiling then headed out of the office. The lights were on in the living room, and he found Allie curled on the couch, reading.

She smiled when she noticed him and set aside the book. "Taking a break?"

"Sorry about that. I think I'm done for the night. Did you eat?"

She shook her head. Brett inclined his toward the kitchen, and she rose. "Where's your sister?"

"Out with friends." He opened the fridge to survey their options for dinner.

"She doesn't seem to like me very much."

Brett sighed. Apparently it was a day for tough conversations. He shut the fridge and turned around. "It's not you. She just takes a while, to warm up to new people."

Allie nodded, dropping her gaze.

"You need to be patient with her," Brett added, more aggressively than he'd intended.

Her lips tightened. Brett's stomach knotted.

"I don't—I don't think it's her. Many… I'm not that likable."

His shoulders actually dropped with the release of tension, and he leaned against the fridge. "Hey." Anxious eyes looked back at him. "I like you."

That didn't have the desired effect. "Her opinion matters to you."

"Yeah. But I think you two will get along pretty well, given the chance." *Hopefully.*

She nodded again, but her eyes didn't relax completely.

"Rough day?"

A slower nod answered.

Brett came to her and took her hands in his. "How about I pour us some wine, find something we don't have to cook for dinner, and we just relax."

Her lips stretched a bit, dropped, and then smiled in earnest. Brett couldn't resist ducking down for a kiss. Vicky was right. He really did like her.

"Someone's looking for you," Wanda announced, handing an order off to Lenny. Allie replaced her time card before following her out. Vic was waiting by the swinging door. Allie hadn't seen her since the previous morning.

"Figured you could use a ride."

"Thank you." Blank politeness had to be a safe bet. She waved at Wanda as they left.

"So, how was work?"

"Pretty usual. How was your day?"

"Uneventful. Did some sketches." They slid into the car, but Vic held on to the keys. "Okay, so, I had an ulterior motive in picking you up," she added before Allie could comment.

"Ulterior motive?" She genuinely intended to approach Vic with cautious amiability, but the phrasing was rather ominous.

"I was thinking we could make dinner tonight, so Brett doesn't have to."

Oh. "That sounds like a wonderful idea. I don't know anything about cooking, though. I would be happy to help however I can."

"I don't really know how to cook, either. Should we get pizza or Chinese?"

Allie exhaled, relaxing somewhat. Perhaps Brett had been right, and the ice was starting to melt. "Which did you miss more?"

"There's actually really good pizza in Paris, so Chinese food I guess." She twisted the key inserted in the car.

"What was your favorite part of your time away?" Allie asked, seizing the opportunity to move beyond the barrier between them.

"Oh, wow, I couldn't choose. It's so different than here. There's art everywhere, incredible exhibits in the city or a train ride away. And I could just sit and draw in the Louvre, surrounded by masterpieces. It was amazing. Not like here."

"Would you want to return?"

"Well, Brett's here. And I've gotta finish my degree."

"And afterward?" Allie asked, genuinely interested in this facet of mortal life. Did they frequently change locations? Vic was quite forthcoming today, though presumably none of this was particularly personal. Still, Allie welcomed the friendly change, even if it was only superficial.

"I dunno. It depends, I guess, on what kind of work I find."

"In addition to your art?"

"Well, yeah. Can't live off Brett forever, not that he wouldn't let me. But he's been taking care of me long enough. That's why I'm also getting a business admin minor."

Their arrival at the restaurant removed the need for a coherent response. After learning that Allie had never eaten Chinese cuisine, Vic handled all of the ordering, selecting an assortment of dishes. As they waited, Allie withdrew the bills Brett had insisted she keep. How astronomical would the charge for such an order be?

"Oh, I got it," Vic offered, seeing the folded bills.

"No, please. I would like to contribute."

"All right, cool. Well, thanks."

The awkwardness persisted as they paid—significantly less than Allie had expected—and returned to the car, laden with bags of food in strangely shaped containers.

Allie had seen similar containers before, crusted with old food, scattered within charges' workplaces. It was disgusting. Presumably the fresh, hot version they had purchased would be superior. Sustenance she had noticed in China itself had consisted primarily of plain rice. This order, mysterious as it was, certainly wasn't that basic, and if anything, she had learned to trust Brett's discernment with food. Hopefully his sister shared that trait, especially since the contents of these cartons were intended for him.

"Hey." Vicky hit the door to his office, and Brett jerked in his seat.

"Hey," he said without turning around.

"You wanna take a break, have dinner?"

"Yeah." He glanced at the clock on the screen. He'd gotten

pretty wrapped up in writing after his run. He was finally back in the groove. "Is Allie back?"

"Yep. How's it coming?"

"Not bad." He rubbed his eyes, trying to massage away the gritty feeling. "I think it might be a leftover kind of night. Or we could order in."

"Way ahead of you. Don't forget to save," she added before walking away.

Brett tapped his fingers on the desk and squinted at the screen, rereading the last words he'd typed. He finished the paragraph and closed out the file. Dinner sounded good, though alcohol might be required to make sure everyone survived. Even if Vicky wasn't technically twenty-one yet.

A line of unmarked white cartons stretched across the kitchen island. Allie set out a stack of plates, and Vicky brought down some glasses.

Allie smiled when she saw him. "Hi."

"Hey." He would've walked over for a proper hello, but he didn't want the homey bubble to burst.

"Don't hold back on my account," Vicky said drily, reading him with ease.

Brett's eyes rolled, but he approached the island anyway. His hands landed effortlessly on Allie's waist. Her head tilted up to his. "Hi."

"You said that already," she pointed out.

"Yeah?" He brushed her lips with his.

"All right, let's eat before I lose my appetite," Vicky muttered. Her mouth pulled into a half smile when he glanced over.

Vicky had gone a bit overboard, so there was way too much food left. But the tension between her and Allie had apparently dissipated, no alcohol required, and the leftovers would keep. Brett cleared the table while they closed up the cartons.

"So, I guess I should get out of your guys' way," Vicky offered uncomfortably once everything was in the fridge.

"Oh, are you tired? I thought, perhaps, we could play cards or something," Allie said without skipping a beat.

Brett could have kissed her right then, not that he needed a reason. "Just as long as we don't play Egyptian Ratscrew."

"Why?" Vicky asked, her shoulders dropping into a slouch.

"Allie's pretty much unbeatable."

"Yeah?" A mischievous grin slowly spread across Vicky's face. Brett groaned.

Sure enough, he was soon watching them battle it out over a fluctuating pile of cards. They'd moved the glass coffee table out of the way and played on the living room rug. Every so often, Brett attempted to slap in, but he didn't want to smack either of them, which seriously impeded his efforts.

"Maybe I should go write, let you two duke it out."

"Yes!" Vicky cried and gathered up the cards piled before them. "You know you couldn't get anything done with us out here."

"We could play something else," Allie offered diplomatically, flipping a new card onto the floor.

"No, no. Far be it from me to get in the way of whatever this is."

Allie looked at him quizzically. "The game?"

Vicky slapped the double sixes unchallenged. "How is your writing going?" she asked, picking up the cards.

"Not terribly." Cards kept flipping almost automatically. "How're those new supplies working out?"

"Actually, I got kind of inspired today. Finished a few sketches."

"Oh! Do you know Nate?" Allie asked.

"Nate?" Vicky echoed. Neither girl looked away from the cards.

"An artist who hangs out at Dreams to Dishes," Brett explained.

"He's having a show on Friday," Allie added.

"Oh yeah? Are you guys going?"

Vicky's three landed on a jack. Allie gathered the small pile and looked to Brett. "That's the plan," he confirmed.

"You should consider going," Allie invited.

"Uhm, sure. Could be fun."

Double tens topped the pile. Their hands snaked out almost simultaneously. Allie's landed on the bottom.

"Nice," Vicky acknowledged. "Are you working Friday?"

"Until three."

"Oh. Well, we could go out, do some girly stuff before the show."

"Since when do you do girly stuff?" Brett asked, though it was surprisingly sweet of her to offer.

"Since it's been more than five months since I got a manicure." She actually paused in the card flipping. "And I'm sure your hands get banged up waitressing, right?"

Allie examined her hands. "I suppose."

"And Brett will totally sponsor us getting some pampering, won't you?" Vicky grinned with fake innocence.

"You bet." Far be it from him to get in the way of female bonding rituals.

❖ ❖ ❖

Allie slipped her jeans off almost as soon as she entered the bedroom. The restrictive fabric bothered her less now, but after a full day bound by it, removing the clothing was still a relief.

"Mind if I join you?" Brett asked from the doorway.

Allie brushed her hair away from her face and smiled. Brett approached and brought her closer for a kiss.

"Thank you," he murmured, still holding her hips.

"For what?" She brought her hands to his shoulders.

"Being cool with my sister."

"Your sister is nice, and quite interesting. When not startled by my presence." As a matter of fact, the siblings had that in common.

"Yeah, she's turned out okay."

"You must have been quite influential, particularly if your parents were not involved." Both of them had hinted at their parents' absence, and Allie's inquisitiveness urged her to mention it. Perhaps Brett would be less reticent about them tonight.

"Our grandparents helped a lot." He stepped away to shut the door. "This actually used to be their house." He drew her to the bed and continued to hold her hand as he spoke. "But they were older, you know? And Vicky was my responsibility, but I couldn't have done it without them."

The nuances of what he had confided eluded her. The concept of raising subsequent generations which had to grow into a functional maturity was entirely of this realm. He spoke of their grandparents as though they lived no longer, which was entirely possible among mortals. Still, one piece seemed fairly certain. "You would have found a way to provide for her, for both of you, as you have been."

His fingers flexed in hers, and he sighed. "Taking care of Vicky has been the most important thing in my life."

"More important than your writing?" Artists of all types frequently prioritized their work over their relationships, except when those relationships were necessary to fuel the art. Creation consumed them.

"Of course. More important than anything." His hand shifted so his thumb rested on her palm. "Or anyone."

Allie looked away from the intensity of his gaze. The message was clear. It shouldn't have affected her, given the temporary nature of her presence in his world. His unyielding affection for his sister was endearing. And yet, some traitorous part of her wished for him to want her to remain a part of his life, to prioritize her the way he did his sister. "Is that why you haven't formed a permanent relationship with a woman?"

He traced the symbol for infinity—a delicate caress in her palm. "With any woman who has been in my life," he said, slowly and deliberately, "I knew that, if I had to, I would always choose Vicky. And I didn't mind."

Allie couldn't form words, so she nodded.

"But with you," he continued, drawing her gaze back to him. "I don't know exactly what it is about you, but I'm incredibly glad that I don't have to choose."

The air seemed to still in her lungs, before her body remembered the need to expel it. Brett's thumb continued its endless loop on her skin. He watched her anticipatorily as his words sank into her.

"Me too," Allie breathed, silently wondering what effect the admission would have on either of their destinies. Then Brett was kissing her, and she no longer cared.

Chapter 19

Brett hadn't figured out the story of the sensual nighttime redhead, so he had no idea what direction to send Pete in. He *had* figured out the reason behind Pete's exhaustion and surety their affair had been only dreams: a rare, active sleepwalking disorder. Sixty-eight cases existed of murder while sleepwalking, and neither Pete nor Brett knew if the detective was about to become number sixty-nine. They didn't even know if the redhead was dead.

It was as good a place to stop as any. He closed out the file and stretched. Gnawing hunger suddenly made itself known, freed from the distraction of his writing, and Brett headed out of his office. On the plus side, they had plenty of leftovers.

He stopped by Vicky's room to see if she'd already eaten. When he opened the door, drying watercolors placed around her room stole his words. Images of Allie amidst flowers and other foliage, walking through a forest, or talking to the flowers surrounded him. It was almost like she'd plucked the visuals from his mind and brought them to life with her art.

Vicky twisted away from her easel, exposing a close-up of Allie. "Uh, hey."

Brett couldn't speak yet.

Vicky set down her brush. "I wanted to have a few more done before I talked to you."

Brett forced his focus away from the paintings. "You hungry? I was going to grab some lunch."

"Sure." She watched him carefully.

Brett spun away and walked to the kitchen. The resemblance of her work to his imaginings was uncanny. Apparently Allie inspired everyone who met her, though he should have been the last one surprised by that.

"Are you mad?" Vicky asked as he pulled Chinese food from the fridge.

"Mad?"

"That I illustrated your story."

Brett shut the fridge and looked at his sister. In her pajamas and with her hair pulled back, she looked no older than fifteen. Her eyes, widened with unfounded concern, didn't help.

"I was going to tell you, I just wanted to have something to show you when I did. You did base the character off Allie, right?"

"Yeah. Wait, you read that story?" He'd almost forgotten about the short, idyllic piece.

She shrugged. "I didn't think you'd mind."

"I don't." That's why he had a password-protected folder, for anything she shouldn't read. "I just didn't realize." The resemblance made more sense now. Remembering himself, Brett went to the cupboard to pull out plates.

Vicky grabbed silverware and started opening the cartons on the island.

"So what did you want to tell me?" Brett asked, plopping some sweet-and-sour chicken onto his plate.

"Well, so, I got an idea, when I read your story. I mean, I'd already seen Allie, so she popped into my mind, but the images were just so vivid. I had to paint them."

Brett smiled wryly. The need to capture Allie on paper wasn't new to him.

"So, I was thinking," Vicky continued, "this could make a pretty great children's book. I mean, I don't know if they turned out the way you saw it, and I could change any of the ones you don't like, but—"

"No," Brett cut off the jittery flow of words. "They're perfect."

Vicky smiled and reached for the fried rice. "So, you think we could publish it? Your story, my pictures. I think I've even worked out my signature: Vic, but with a capital *K* instead of the *c*, because of Knightley? Get it?"

Brett rolled his eyes at her enthusiasm. "Yeah, I got it." He took her plate over to the microwave and set it heating. "But, Vicky, you know children's publishing is an entirely separate world from what I do. It has different rules, different agents, everything. Sean doesn't rep children's books, and I'm not all that sure my story is what a children's agent would be looking for, anyway."

"Well, yeah. But Sean probably knows some people, right? And it couldn't hurt to shop it around, or pitch it, or whatever."

The microwave beeped, and Brett switched their plates. Vicky took hers from him and settled on a barstool. "I don't know, Vicky." Querying was a long and complicated process.

"Don't know what?"

"I haven't even read that story since I wrote it. It's just a draft, and I'm not a children's author."

"Can't we let someone more familiar with that market decide that? Or do you just hate the idea of working together."

Brett took his food from the microwave and rounded the island, settling beside her. "Look, your drawings are amazing." Sure, he was biased, but Vicky was truly talented. "But I'm just not sure where we would even take this, or how this would work. And you know I have a deadline coming up."

"Yeah, by the way, I read that hidden darkness of suburbia opening. Is that all you have? I mean, it's intriguing, I guess, but if that's all you have down, Sean's going to kill you."

"Yeah, thanks." Not that she was wrong. "But I do have something else I'm working on. It's a bit more developed. And that's exactly my point. I don't really have time to branch out into an entirely new category right now."

Vicky twirled her fork in the medley of foods on her plate. "I think it's closer to done than you think. I mean, if you really think my paintings are any good."

"They're incredible. Like you saw exactly what I did."

"Well, see! If I can do that from reading your story, it's clearly not as bad as you think," Vicky stated triumphantly. "Your words created the world, or I wouldn't have been able to draw it."

He couldn't really argue with that, and Vicky knew it. But a children's book author? "Brett Knightley, author of picture books and adult mysteries," he mocked.

Vicky scrunched her nose. "Yeah, you're right. How about, Brick and ViK?"

He arched one eyebrow.

"What? Breck and ViK doesn't sound right."

"Yeah, *that's* the problem."

"Well, we could figure out a children-friendly pseudonym for you later. Look, it's your story, but I really think this is something worth pursuing. What's the worst that could happen?"

"Rejection. Lots and lots of it."

"That's never stopped you before."

"It's not me I'm worried about." He'd already faced the mountains of rejections, but Vicky hadn't. And you really didn't know how it felt until it happened, over and over. He didn't want that for her, if at all possible.

"Oh, come on. I'm not ten years old anymore, Brett. And this is something we could do that's actually together, not just you taking care of me."

The one thing Vicky hadn't forgotten from their time with their parents was how to manipulate people. She could probably get anyone to do just about anything she wanted. Or maybe he was particularly susceptible. Brett sighed, considering his baby sister, who wasn't such a baby anymore.

"At the very least, we should talk to Sean and see what he says," she needled.

"Yeah, all right," he relented. "But I don't want to approach him until I have this other book figured out, okay?"

Vicky grinned then plopped a honey-walnut shrimp in her mouth. Brett shook his head, knowing full well he had no idea what he'd just gotten himself into.

"How about 'after sex'?" Vic asked, holding up a little bottle with a deep-burgundy substance inside.

Allie would have rejected the idea, but the skew of Vic's features clearly demonstrated the suggestion wasn't serious. She smiled in return and pulled another bottle off the shelf. "How about 'delicacy'?"

"Boring," Vic commented melodically and plucked the soft tan from Allie's grasp. Her fingers ran along the shelf, filled predominately with slightly differing shades of red, and stopped at a particularly bright hue of purple. "'DJ play that song'?"

"For you?" The shade was much too adventurous for Allie. All around them sat pairs of women, chatting quietly as one treated the hands of the other. The nails of women who left were invariably painted with colors, which was presumably why she and Vic now stood before the vast selection of tiny, colorful bottles.

"Actually, maybe." Vicky chose a black bottle from the shelf. "With black tips? Could be fun for a few days."

Allie glanced at her own unadorned nails. What a peculiar custom to color them for days at a time. Did mortal women then select their wardrobes to match for the duration of the color? Vic couldn't possibly own an abundance of clothing that could complement such a vibrant purple.

If this is how mortals shared time, however, Allie had little choice but to participate. At least the unnatural smell that had assaulted them when they entered the small business seemed to have faded. Either that, or her ability to smell had been rapidly destroyed.

"I got it!" Vic's exclamation drew Allie out of her contemplation. A pleasant blue, a slightly deeper shade than the sky Allie and Brett had admired on the mountainside, dangled from her fingers. "Parisian blue. I think it's perfect for you."

"Are you certain? It is still a somewhat intense color."

"We're going to an art show, not a funeral. It's just a bit exciting. Plus, Brett loves blue."

Allie's lips pressed into a wry smile. The subtext was quite obvious, even to her. "Is that so?"

Vic's eyebrows shot up over widened eyes as she nodded.

An employee suddenly appeared beside them. "We're all set for you ladies."

Vic firmly planted the blue bottle in Allie's palm and followed the dark-haired woman to a pair of large, black chairs reminiscent of the one in Brett's office. Allie sighed and trailed them, fingering the smooth glass. Thankfully, none of the women around her appeared to be suffering as their color was applied. Allie settled in the chair and watched Vic, mimicking her arm placement on the cushions set before each chair.

Two women, both dressed in long-sleeved, white jackets settled on the other side of the thin table, each lifting one of the girls' hands. Vic didn't react, and Allie attempted to follow suit.

"So. What are your intentions toward my brother?" The casual nonchalance of the question was belied by the piercing attention of Vic's eyes.

Startled, Allie fell back on her ingrained decorum. "How do you mean?"

"Is this just a fling? Or are you one of those girls who believes writers make tons of money."

"Is that truly how I appear to you?"

"That's not an answer." Vic squinted slightly, watching her.

The women treating their hands exchanged glances. Vic either didn't notice or wasn't concerned.

"My relationship with your brother is the most caring and intimate I have ever had. I have never felt about anyone the way I feel about him." Though precisely what those feelings were remained unclear.

"So you think it'll last?"

It can't. "I certainly don't like considering the alternative." She had become nearly complacent in her current state, intensely enjoying Brett's attentions and company. Yet she had no reference for knowing if he returned her growing affections. "There are two individuals involved in any relationship."

"True enough," Vic answered.

Unfortunately, no hint as to Brett's own intentions was forthcoming. It shouldn't have concerned her, but the idea of a future with Brett was oddly tantalizing, despite its impossibility. She should have been focusing on disentangling the spell before she wore out her welcome.

"What about yourself?" Allie asked, shifting the subject away from the jumble this one had created in her mind. "Is there someone with whom you're involved?"

"Not since I got back. But hey, there might always be someone cute there tonight."

They left the salon with their hands massaged and nails expertly painted. The blue on Allie's nails glinted in the sunlight as they enjoyed iced teas and fruit tarts at the single outdoor table of a small pastry shop Vic had insisted they visit. Vic's black-tipped nails were decisively more daring, but that suited her artistic nature. The color even complemented the pink strips in her hair.

"Would you mind if I asked you a question?" Allie ventured, curling her fingers to hide the unnaturally colored ends.

"Shoot."

Presumably that was permission. "Do you miss your parents?"

Vic's head snapped toward her. Thin lines appeared over her nose, and her lips paled from the force of being pressed together. A few moments later, her shoulders dropped. "He hasn't told you about them has he?"

"Solely that they have not been an active presence in your life."

Vic's mouth fell open in a combination of a chuckle and sigh. "That's the understatement of the century." She sipped at her iced tea. "Let's just say they weren't too interested in being parents." Her gaze fell to the table before her. "Sometimes I think they had me just to keep Brett occupied."

Allie couldn't comment. Surely Brett wasn't so significantly older than his sister that he would have been sufficiently capable of caring for an infant.

"They were too busy to really take care of him, so they gave him something to do, and that was taking care of me. Or maybe that wasn't intentional. But he's been taking care of me for as long as I can remember."

"While they were working?" Human parents provided for their progeny, though sometimes the effort of doing so overwhelmed the parents. Allie did know that.

"Yeah, sort of. They flipped houses, on the cheap." Allie's confusion must have been evident, because Vic explained without prompting. "They would buy these rundown places, and fix them up, but not very well. I didn't know that at the time, of course. I thought it was exciting. We'd move somewhere ugly, and then mom and dad would make it beautiful." She looked back down to the table before her, shaking her head. "But they didn't do it up to code or anything, and they'd sell it for way more than it was worth. They could convince anyone to buy just about anything, really. The whole thing rarely took more than a few months, so we'd move around a lot. They might've had some other schemes going too, I don't know. But while they were busy, Brett would feed me, or even take me clothes shopping, to the park, play dates, everything.

"Sometimes, in the summer, we'd come out here and stay with our grandparents. That was the only time we'd have real beds or anything, but I thought camping or sleeping on air mattresses was more fun. Sometimes they'd let me help pick out colors or stuff like that. When I was old enough, I would bake cookies with our mom when they had people coming over to look at the house." She glanced up, smiling tightly.

"What changed?" Allie asked quietly.

"One day, when I was ten, Brett picked me up from school with our duffel bags, put us in a taxi, and took us to the airport. It was early in the school year, so I didn't get it. I never saw our parents again, and honestly I hated him for taking me away from them."

Why would he separate a young child from her parents? *Their* parents? Had some accident befallen them?

"What I didn't know back then," Vic continued, "is that they'd sold our last house and left. Brett had just turned eighteen, and they had packed up our things, leaving them at his school's office, along with papers naming him my legal guardian. They might've left him some cash, too, I don't know. But he couldn't have taken me to them if he wanted to, so he brought us here, to the only real home we'd ever had."

Though the finer details remained beyond Allie's comprehension, the image finally cleared. "He shielded you from the truth."

Brett had made his commitment to his sister perfectly evident, but now Allie saw its roots. He had created a life for her where their parents had not made the effort to do so, even while faced with Vic's childishly innocent loathing. There must have been alternatives, including simply abandoning her as their parents had, but Allie was certain Brett had not even considered those.

Vic watched her for a prolonged moment, her expression beyond Allie's insights. "It took me longer than I'd like to admit he wasn't to blame." She sighed, shaking her head, sending the memories away. "So, are you officially scared?"

"Scared?" Allie parroted.

"A lot of women would be intimidated, knowing he puts me first, whether or not he should."

That information wasn't new to her, but Vic clearly awaited reassurance, her youth strikingly evident in that moment. "I cannot claim to be an expert, but caring for others doesn't seem to be a finite capability. I don't know how your brother feels about me, but his obvious affection for you is certainly not a deterrent." Unlike her being of another realm.

Vic watched her humorlessly, with pursed lips. "For someone who's so good with words, he does suck at saying certain things." Allie would have asked her to elaborate, but Vic stood, ostensibly ending their discussion. "Anyway, we should probably get going if we still want to change for tonight."

Brett should have been figuring out what had happened to the Vixen. Had she been kidnapped? Or killed? Was she herself a con artist, seeking information on the detective's cases for her own nefarious needs? Pete mostly wanted to relive the dreams that had been real, not that Brett could blame him. But that wouldn't get either of them anywhere.

Vicky was out with Allie, and that was all Brett could think about since sending Sean a draft of the first few chapters. If Vicky was actually on board with Allie being around, and not just being polite, there was nothing to worry about. If not, there was a good chance she could get Allie to leave and never look back, which was the last thing Brett wanted. He liked having Allie around. He didn't want to just throw away whatever it was they had, even if she had come to live there out of a bizarre necessity.

That entire mess had worked out unbelievably well. It was almost lucky, not that he believed in luck. She had successfully insinuated herself into his life, but he was past minding. There was an ease to her company that lifted his spirits and refocused his mind, even if that focus was often on lascivious thoughts that could never make it to the page. There was nothing disruptive about her presence. But with Vicky added into the picture, that could easily change.

Best-case scenario, they would get along, and Brett would be outnumbered, though the idea of Allie being a more permanent fixture in their lives was more than appealing.

As if conjured by his mind, her voice came from behind him. "Hi, there."

Brett spun from his computer and took the couple steps toward her. She didn't seem upset, but there was a weird tension in her hands. Sky blue covered her nails. "Did you two have fun?"

"I got her back to you in one piece, didn't I?" Vicky called from down the hall.

Allie exhaled through a chuckle.

Brett took her hands and pulled her in for a kiss as relief swept through him.

"Well you certainly made an impression," Vicky stated as they entered Nate's loft. Both paintings in his entryway featured likenesses of Allie.

Brett wrapped his arm around her waist, feeling a little silly, but she didn't seem to notice the proprietary gesture.

"Who's the blonde, though?" Vicky asked.

"Kristie, one of the waitresses at the diner," Allie explained.

Allie's bright hair made her stand out on the canvases as much as in real life, but on further consideration, it was clear she wasn't the focus of these paintings. One featured her and Kristie behind the bar at the diner. Allie couldn't be painted as anything other than stunning, but Kristie shone, depicted as though the light saw only her, glinting off her pale-gold hair and almost caressing her skin. In the other, Allie was painted behind a seated artist, presumably Nate himself, directing his attention to Kristie as he sketched. Hints of the background also set this in a diner, but most of the walls and furniture hadn't been included, so the focus was on the softly smiling blonde.

Would Allie be jealous not to be the heart of Nate's pieces?

Before Brett could find a way to ask, their host came from somewhere in the back, carrying a tray with cheese cubes, which he set on a table placed out of the way. "Hey. Glad you guys could make it," he greeted upon reaching them.

Brett let go of Allie to shake his proffered hand.

"Thank you for the invitation," Allie said politely.

"Not at all. Do you, uh, did Kristie say anything to you? About coming?"

"She doesn't work on Fridays," Allie pointed out apologetically.

"Right. No, of course. I knew that." Nate turned to Vicky. "I'm sorry, I'm being so rude. Welcome." He glanced among them for an introduction.

"This is my sister, Vicky."

"Vic," she corrected instantly.

"Nate." He smiled and spread his arms, gesturing around the loft. "Please, enjoy. And I would love to hear your thoughts."

"Careful," Brett warned, more for Vicky's sake than Nate's.

"Am I missing something?" the artist asked. "Will I need armor before the night is through?"

"Depends," Vicky piled on.

Nate glanced between them, bemused.

"Vic is also an artist," Allie explained graciously.

"Well, I'm studying."

"Oh great!" Nate smiled a bit more genuinely. "Well, then, I look forward to you ripping me to shreds."

"Guess I should sharpen my claws, then," Vicky said with a smile that wasn't quite as sweet as Brett would have liked.

"I seem to have been warned," Nate said conspiratorially. "Since you're here, let me introduce you to some people."

Vicky followed him without hesitation, leaving Allie and Brett to explore the small show alone. The loft had been well set up, not overcrowded with paintings, really utilizing the space to show off as many as possible. Maybe ten people total filled the empty spaces, giving a similar feel of saturation without crowding.

"So what do you think?" Brett asked when they'd made it halfway around the room. Every piece they'd seen so far featured Kristie in one manner or another.

"I truly hope Kristie comes. It is quite evident how deeply he cares for her, looking at these."

"You don't mind?" Brett asked, keeping his tone casual.

"Mind?"

"That you're not his inspiration for these." Would she realize he was jealous?

That pulled her attention from the painting before them. "I am perfectly content with not being the subject of his paintings. The intimacy of his affection for Kristie seems to have been the impetus for this collection."

"So you're okay with not being his muse? So to speak."

"Perhaps I am, if that painting in the entryway is to be believed." She flashed a small smile, obviously waiting for his response.

"Well, mythologically, muses were responsible for the inspiration of artists. They were the source of the work. 'Speak to me, oh muse,' and all that. Kristie is obviously his inspiration for these."

"Perhaps human mythology isn't a reflection of the reality."

"Of course not, since muses in the mythological sense don't actually exist."

"That isn't what I meant." She stepped toward the next painting, shifting her attention to it. "Perhaps mythology which teaches that muses are co-creators, or simply utilize mortals for the creation of their own works, is wrong, not in that muses do not exist, but in that their role is different."

A trio of Nate's guests moved around them, and Brett shifted to let them pass. He stepped behind Allie and placed his hands on her hips, drawing her in against him. "So what, then? Muses divert our attention?"

"What if they enhance the inclination to produce? They could guide the process of realizing an idea, ensuring that process fulfills its potential rather than placing the ideas themselves in your head."

"Then centuries of diviners would have been wrong," he teased.

Allie's head turned so she could see him over her shoulder. She considered him briefly before stepping away, toward the next painting. "Stranger things have happened," she murmured.

"It's an idea," Brett agreed, trailing after her. "Muses inspiring production more so than directing a subject."

"Consider the limit of muses. If there were less than ten, as mythology suggests, wouldn't all of the work created center predominately on similar subjects and themes?"

"Well sure, but isn't that an argument against the idea of mythological rather than temporary, mortal muses as inspiration?" They continued their slow circle of the loft.

"Or one contradicting the dominant view on mythological muses' role," she corrected, sticking to her theory. She seemed strangely sure.

Brett smiled. It was nice to see her so confident. "Do you know something the rest of us don't?"

Allie's gaze jumped to his face. She smiled enigmatically rather than answer. Would it be inappropriate to kiss her here?

Chapter 20

Vicky's appearance beside them prevented him from deciding. "Okay, you have to see this," she claimed, pulling Allie away. Brett smiled and followed. At least they were getting along.

They stopped in front of a medium-sized canvas. Allie froze, her pale skin lending itself to the illusion of her becoming statuesque. Brett glanced at the painting and blanked. He shook his head as if that could dislodge the canvas from its easel.

The painting was split horizontally into two parts. The lower featured an art studio, strewn with paints and mostly blank canvases, except a finished one in the corner. The upper part was all Allie, waist-deep in a lake, naked except for the lush waves of hair that curled over her shoulders and demurely over and around her breasts. Regaining some semblance of a mind, Brett stepped in front of the painting, blocking it from view.

Allie's stunned expression warred in his mind with the painted image.

"I'm sorry. I didn't," Vicky stammered. "I thought you would've known."

"I did not," Allie breathed.

"But, it's beautiful, how he painted you..." She trailed off at

Brett's sharp look but soon shot him her own frustrated one. "Are you upset he used you for his art? Without asking you?"

Allie inhaled and looked at Vicky.

Damn it. Without realizing it, he'd done the same thing, or maybe even worse, just no one had seen it yet. And through his story, Vicky had, too.

"No, that is the artist's right," Allie said. "I was merely surprised."

Brett let out the breath he must've been holding, grateful Vicky had asked the question he couldn't.

"But, look at it," Vicky continued, refocusing on the painting. "I mean, if Brett would *move*, it's almost like he painted you in another realm. The different color palates, and even the strokes are harder in the artist's world than in the one he made for you. I don't think it was meant to be inappropriate, or anything."

They both looked to Allie.

"No, that does not seem likely," she agreed.

Brett took her hand in his, lacing their fingers together as his thumb traced patterns on her palm.

Vicky pressed on. "Don't get me wrong, I mean, he obviously loves that Kristie chick. But this. It's almost like he's worshipping you. Like you're the one who gave him his art."

"Or gave it back," Brett added without thinking. Allie's fingers tightened for a second in his.

"You see all of that in this piece?" she asked Vicky.

"Well, unlike the two of you," his sister said, looking mostly at him, "I actually looked at it for more than a couple seconds. But, yeah."

Allie relaxed under the reprimand, even smiling slightly. "I suppose you're right. Neither of us afforded this painting the attention it is due."

"So, if it's exploitative but for the sake of art, it's okay?" Brett asked, needing to hear more of her thoughts on the topic. At least if she said no, he could erase the file before it saw the light of day, tell Sean to forget about it. Or change the details of the Vixen.

"It isn't exploitative," Allie countered. "I was surprised, but that isn't why. I am simply unaccustomed to being quite so visible."

She tugged on their joined hands, pulling Brett away from the painting. He stepped forward reluctantly, twisting so his back still shielded it somewhat from the rest of the room. Looking at the painting more closely, he could kind of see the contrasts Vicky had mentioned, but his eyes kept going to Allie's painted form.

"See?" Vicky said quietly. "She's untouchable here. Beyond the artist's reach, or the mortal world, or however you want to see it.

Allie's eyes narrowed as she contemplated the painting. Vicky's interpretation made an odd kind of sense, even when he looked at the live version. "She's definitely something special," Brett murmured. He hadn't seen the first painting since she'd brought it home, but the question hadn't changed. Could he blame the other man for seeing Allie? For being driven to create by her, just like he had been? For that matter, just like Vicky had?

"Okay, you've gotten cloyingly sweet," Vicky said, breaking the tension that had built around them. "And way too cliché."

"She's incomparably incandescent," Brett shot back.

"Trying too hard," Vicky said with a smirk.

Allie blushed adorably. "Enough! I am not the point. Nate must have put significant effort into bringing this evening together, and we should be appreciating his work and his talent."

"Agreed, though this one is still one of my favorites so far. I'm going to go look around some more," Vicky announced and crossed the room without waiting for a reply.

Brett pulled Allie closer. "You're really okay with him using you in his work?" he asked, mostly to assuage his own guilt.

"I don't interpret it as him taking advantage in any way. Truly," she assured.

Brett lowered his voice. "Would I be taking advantage? Imagining you coming out of a lake like that, toward me?"

Her lips parted just enough that they were no longer pressed together. Brett brushed his thumb over the inside of her wrist. She shivered lightly.

"Have I told you how beautiful you look tonight?"

She smiled, eyes flicking down shyly. He leaned down to catch her curved lips in a not-quite-chaste kiss, propriety be damned.

Allie awoke alone. She swept an arm out, brushing the sheets beside her until she reached the second pillow. With her eyes shut against the light, she sat up, sorting through the previous night's memories.

Kristie had in fact arrived at Nate's show, and Allie had seen him lead her around the temporary gallery. The three of them had left soon afterward, though Brett hadn't been particularly happy about leaving the one painting behind.

Vic had convinced Brett to drop her off somewhere. Allie and Brett had returned alone, and he had certainly accompanied her to the bedroom. The returning memory sent brushes of sensation through her. She blew her breath out and threw off the covers.

She didn't remember Brett leaving, but she refused to dwell on the lack of his arms around her this morning. She had no reason to expect him to spend each of her days off together. Perhaps he was writing, and if so, she should have been encouraging his progress, not lamenting his absence. She had wholly lost sight of her true purpose, not to mention of the supposedly pressing issue of returning to her true form.

She dressed quickly then stepped into the bathroom to perform the morning rituals that had already become routine. Presumably, if she were to spend the day alone, she could explore Brett's library. Or, perhaps, finally untangle the cause of her transformation enough to find the loophole, though that would likely require more than a day.

She would have preferred to spend it enjoying Brett, and not solely in a physical way, though that was certainly surpassingly appealing. Merely being in his company somehow calmed and delighted her at once, as though he shielded her from the tumultuous questions and emotions raging within, while bathing her in the contented knowledge that he did, in fact, see her. And like her, significantly more than any of her own peers.

Still deep in thought, she stepped into the hallway.

"You're up," Brett's dismayed voice greeted her. He stood shirtless in the corridor, holding a tray laden with dishes and a lovely gardenia. "I was going to bring you breakfast in bed."

"Thank you," Allie said reflexively as her heart thumped. The knowledge that he had wanted to spend at least the morning with her made her oddly giddy.

Brett watched her without comment.

"Have you eaten?" she added, unsure how else to salvage the plan she'd inadvertently disrupted.

A small smile twitched his lips. "Breakfast for two," he said, lifting the tray slightly. "But I could take it back to the kitchen, if you want."

"Whatever you would prefer."

His eyes trailed down her body as though seeing beyond her clothing. "Well, the bedroom would give us a bit more privacy."

"You did go through such an effort." She moved closer to the bedroom door, forgetting everything but the opportunity of more time with this man, a mortal who shouldn't have mattered yet affected her beyond anything she could verbalize.

He walked toward her then past her into the room, where he set the tray on the bed. With his hands freed, he approached her and pulled her close, murmuring, "Good morning."

Allie smiled into his kiss. When they drew back, the fluttering of the leaves outside created the illusion of the sun itself winking at them through the window. Brett reached behind her and shut the door.

"This would work better if you were back in bed."

"Should I..." She didn't finish the question. Undressing for the sake of eating felt silly, though she did still prefer avoiding mortal cloth.

His fingers snuck under the hem of her top. "I could help you get more comfortable," he offered.

She splayed her fingers on his chest, relishing the warm feel of his skin. His thumbs brushed her sides below the fabric then around to the front of her jeans. The band loosened, and Allie slid her palms up to his shoulders. Brett's hands moved down her hips and to her bottom, pushing the pants to the floor. Allie pressed on his frame to kick the jeans free. Brett's fingers traced up her spine, and she arched into him.

"Won't breakfast grow cold?"

Brett's head turned toward the tray, and he groaned. "Yeah." He grabbed the hem of her top, and she lifted her arms from him, expecting him to fling the fabric free. He peeled it off but then tangled it around her hands, trapping them. Before Allie could question it, he covered her lips with his, brushing softly until she hummed in response.

He tugged her toward the bed before tossing the top away, then picked up the small pitcher of juice on the tray. Allie scooted onto the bed, careful not to dislodge the breakfast he'd prepared. A heap of eggs, scrambled with whatever he had added, overwhelmed the single plate. He had included a small bowl of fruit.

Brett filled the two glasses beside it and offered her one of the forks. Allie tasted the eggs as he settled near her, weaving the fingers of her free hand in his.

"So, what do you want to do today?"

"I'm happy right here," Allie answered without thinking. The truth of those words quickly caught up to her. She had on occasion vicariously experienced the triumph of success through her charges, and yet that didn't compare to the contentment of simply being there, with Brett.

He grinned at her and picked up the other fork.

Could she spend a mortal lifetime here with him? Would he even consider that an option? "And you? What would you like to do today?"

"Oh believe me, I'm more than happy here." He shifted their joined hands to her bare lap.

"You don't need to work?"

"Well, I probably should, but I'd rather be with you."

She opened her mouth to protest, and he slipped his fork, generously laden with eggs, in to stop her.

"It can wait," he assured. "We could stay—" A melody emanating from his pocket interrupted him. "Sorry." He lowered his fork and reached into his pocket, then frowned at the small device. "It's Sean, my agent. I have to take this."

"Of course." It was astounding how rapidly mortal communication devices progressed.

He smiled at her then unbent the contraption. "Hey, Sean."

Allie sipped some juice as he waited.

"No, no, it's fine. Is something wrong? I didn't think you'd get to those pages so quickly." He lifted their hands to his mouth, brushing hers with a kiss before letting go to leave the bed.

Chapter 21

"Wait, what?"

"You know, the short story Vicky came to see me about yesterday. I've gotta say, I wasn't expecting it."

"Yeah, neither was I." Vicky had been gone all day yesterday before meeting up with Allie, but he hadn't considered the possibility that she'd driven out to Denver. Come to think of it, she hadn't actually agreed to wait to show Sean the pages.

"Those sketches were really something, huh? The story wasn't bad, but you know, it's not my thing. Vicky told me you were on board, so I did send it out to a couple people I know when she left."

"Oh yeah?" Brett steeled himself. Despite Vicky's faith, he knew children's books weren't in his wheelhouse. Like with other genres, people spent ages perfecting the right tone, learning that specific market. He was a mystery writer, and purely for adults. For that matter, Sean's willingness to contact other agents on his behalf was unusual to say the least, though Vicky was nothing if not convincing.

"Yeah, well. I've gotta tell you." Sean paused, probably trying to pick his words. "I've already heard back from someone, and she sounds pretty interested. They loved Vicky's pictures, the concept. It doesn't sound like you, but apparently it worked for them. So I can arrange some meetings, but we'll have to discuss how this'll work. I mean, is it just a one-off for you?"

"I, uh. I don't know. Probably." Brett turned from the window to look at Allie. "Maybe."

"Well, it's definitely something to think about. But I'm glad to see you're still working away at those mysteries. That deadline is coming up sooner than you know it."

"Yeah, listen…"

"So I did glance at those pages already." *Unbelievable.* The turnaround was unprecedented. "And I've gotta say, that must be quite some redhead you've found. This is nothing like the Brett Knightley the world has seen, but in a great way. It's still rough of course, lots of work left to do. But this should give us a solid place to negotiate this option, maybe make it a multi-book deal. It is a little risky to go with something so new, so different, but you know, I like it, I think this could work. The next phase of your career."

"That's great. I'm glad you liked them." It really was. He'd worried about the departure, but between Allie's assurance last night that being reinterpreted in art wasn't exploitative and Sean's enthusiasm, he was actually starting to think this book could turn out okay. If he ever figured out where it was going.

Sean kept rattling off plans and details, and Brett tuned back in. "Can talk about it in person," the agent was saying. "I can do Tuesday, say about three. Can you make it out here?"

It was only about a half-hour drive, and Sean was asking mostly as a courtesy. Allie would be at the diner, so it could easily work. "Yeah, that sounds good, Sean."

"All right, great, buddy. I'll see you then. You enjoy your weekend."

"See ya." He slipped the phone back in his pocket and focused on the woman on his bed, who was watching him, resting against the pillows with the flower he'd picked in her hands and her legs stretched out before her, crossed at the ankles. He still had no idea how she'd come into his life, but he was way past caring. She was incredible, in bed, out of it, and even on paper. And he was damn lucky she was there. "Sorry about that."

She slid off the bed to stand beside him. "Was it good news?"

"Yeah, actually." His arms circled her waist. Her hands effortlessly came to his biceps. "There's this story I wrote, that Vicky decided to illustrate. She showed it all to my agent yesterday, and he seemed surprisingly enthusiastic about it."

A bright smile appeared without hesitation. "That's wonderful!"

"He also said he liked the pages I sent him, which is a relief. They're not exactly my usual style."

"Experimentation is frequently rewarded in the arts, if well executed."

"Ah, thanks. I have to tell you, though." Her smile lessened expectantly. "Both are, uh. They're kind of about you, or reimagined versions of you."

"Of—of me?"

"Yeah. You really did inspire me, in every way." He bent to kiss her, tasting the faint traces of orange juice in her mouth and sliding his hands up to her ribcage, below the fall of her hair. *The food's still on the bed*, he remembered. He pulled back then brushed her lips with his once more, before stepping away to get rid of the tray. He didn't take it far, leaving it out of the way to be cleaned up later, then came to take both of her hands in his.

She watched him with the hints of sultry knowledge that had grown in her eyes over their time together.

"You know," Brett said, "if muses really do exist, you're definitely mine."

A fresh, broader smile curved her lips, and she tilted her chin up for a kiss. A blink later, he was alone.

Brett glanced around his bedroom, shaking the slightly foggy feeling from his brain. "Allie?" The tray still stood in the corner. The bed was still unmade. "Allie?" A matching set of bra and panties stared dully back at him.

Allie couldn't speak. It had taken her a moment to comprehend his confusion, but then she'd felt the spark of power return to her. She closed her eyes and waited for the sense of relief that should have accompanied the transformation, the return to her natural form, but all she felt was bereft of the mortal before her who had come to mean too much. She should have already returned to faerie, but leaving him was inconceivable.

A knock on the door pulled Brett's focus. "Yeah," he called sharply.

"Hey, I thought I heard you up," Vic said, opening the door. "Can I... What's up?" She looked around the room. "Where's Allie?"

Brett's gaze snapped back to his sister.

Allie saw him swallow, then exhale.

"She's gone." He stepped to the bed, sinking down on the edge.

"I thought she didn't have work today?"

"That's not what I meant."

Vic walked further into the room, sharp eyes taking in the tray of food and muss of the bedspread. "What did you mean?"

"That she's gone. Off to con some other unwitting sap who's too distracted by her innocent act to remember he knows better." His hands clenched, bulging the muscles in his arms.

Vic stayed silent.

Allie fled.

Chapter 22

Brett's eyes fell back to the bed, to the lingerie that shouldn't have been there. He stood and stalked out of his room.

"What are you doing?" Vicky trailed behind him toward the kitchen.

"Getting a garbage bag." How could he have been so stupid! Falling for the stranger who'd come out of nowhere. *Not her, her act.*

"Brett. Hang on a second."

He spun to face his sister. He'd failed yet again to protect her from a con artist. "I'm sorry."

Vicky crossed her arms over her chest. "You're being ridiculous."

"I know, I should have known better."

"Allie wouldn't leave, just like that." She snapped her fingers for emphasis.

That's exactly how she'd appeared. But Vicky didn't need to know that. How could he explain the incomprehensible? Before Vicky'd asked about Allie, he'd thought he might have made her up—a vivid hallucination. At least he wasn't completely nuts, just an idiot.

"Brett, listen to me. She really cares about you."

A tiny part of him whispered that Vicky read people well. But then, usually, so did he.

"I think she even loves you, she just hasn't realized it yet." Vicky hadn't idealized people since she'd learned the truth about their parents, but she was young, and far from infallible. "And I'm pretty sure you love her, though that's not the point."

Brett sighed, feeling the span of the years between them in a way he hadn't since he'd first brought them here. "What is your point, Vicky?"

"She wouldn't just leave. I'm sure of it. I know having faith in people isn't exactly something you're good at, but trust me. And if you can't do that, just think about it."

"It's not about trusting you, Vicky. She fooled both of us."

"And got what, exactly? I mean, look around." Her arms gestured widely toward the living room, drawing his attention. "Nothing's missing. I bet if you checked your wallet, everything would still be there, too. Hell, she insisted on paying for the Chinese food! Not exactly a brilliant deceptive move."

Brett tried to still his mind enough to think through Vicky's point. His book wasn't even finished yet, so that couldn't be what Allie'd been after—and there were easier ways to steal someone's manuscript. Despite his protests, she had insisted on paying him back for the clothes he'd bought, by working as a waitress, which wasn't exactly a get-rich-quick scheme. And it wasn't like she'd taken the clothes with her, which he didn't even try to figure out. His gaze came to the bookshelves that had, of everything in his home, most fascinated her. Not a single book was missing.

"You're right," he conceded, leaning against the wall in defeat and passing a hand over his face. "I just don't know what happened." His mind was back to blank, unable to weave the pieces together cohesively.

"Well, I'm telling you," Vicky said stubbornly, "wherever she went, she'll be back."

Allie knelt on the earth before Matera. The act of deference was a custom adopted long ago from the mortal realm, which she had only now come to appreciate fully. Maintaining such a position in that realm would undoubtedly be progressively more painful as time went on, a cruelty she and her kind were spared.

"You were foolish, Alexandra. Imprudent, impulsive, disrespectful." Matera's words were harsher than her tone. She paced in a thin oval as she spoke. "What came over you? Such reckless disregard for your duty and powers beyond your own isn't at all like you. If it weren't for Liliana, who knows what may have befallen you?"

So she hadn't imagined the glimmer of a sprite's magic. Allie pressed her lips together, maintaining the downward tilt of her head. Her behavior may not have been customary, but hadn't she yearned for something beyond duty for centuries? The fae realm had previously been all she had known. Unsuited as she had always felt to it, it had always been her home. Now… Now, she was back. She would have to find the sprite to express her gratitude for the assistance.

"Perhaps I have been sending you too frequently into the mortal world." Matera sighed. "Perhaps it would do well for you to spend more time among your own kind, to temper your fury for the mortals."

"My time among the mortals has done so already." Matera's skirts stilled before her. "I know my place, Matera." Inspiring those like Nate and Brett, even Vicky, would fulfill her, despite not being accepted by her colleagues and continuing to be disregarded by her charges. That was the role for which she existed, regardless of the simple pleasures discovered in her time in the mortal realm, of the moments whose meaning Brett had stolen the instant she had regained her true form.

She had no place in his world.

Matera sighed again. "Rise, Alexandra." She strode to her verdant throne, woven from living plants. She lowered gracefully then gestured beside herself. Instantly, new life grew into a stool.

Allie had never received such an intimate invitation from the leader of the fae, but she knew it could not be declined. The stool continued to grow around her once she sat, transforming into a chair molded to her shape. A fresh gardenia bloom worked its way between her fingers. Allie snatched her hand away from the reminder of her witless idealism.

"You are aware of the occasional losses among us," Matera stated.

Allie dipped her chin though there was no question.

Matera stroked the varied blooms that stretched to her from beneath the throne. "'Not all those who wander are lost.' A beautiful line in its simplicity, is it not? Lacking the permanence of home does not automatically mean one isn't precisely where one is intended to be."

"I have missed the splendors of our home," Allie said cautiously, unable to read Matera's intentions.

"It is a mortal saying, inspired by one of your friends."

Colleagues, Allie corrected silently. The closest she had ever had to friends lived in the mortal realm. Or so she had come to believe. Would they, too, now denounce her?

"What you must consider, Alexandra, is that not all those who find their way back are able to move forward."

For the first time since her return, Allie's gaze met Matera's. Her unparalleled eyes shifted colors as only they were able. A slight curve graced the flawless plumpness of her lips. Matera held her gaze for less than a mortal minute before turning away and gesturing to her arched entryway.

Allie stood, recognizing the dismissal despite her murky comprehension of the cryptic comment. She bent her knees, dipping toward the ground before turning away. Muses could transport themselves anywhere, but encroaching upon Matera's space by appearing or disappearing at will was the height of incivility, so she strode silently through Matera's garden to the marble.

"Oh, and, Alexandra," Matera called from behind her. Allie spun around respectfully, ducking her head. "He remains your charge."

Brett couldn't figure it out. He'd turned the pieces he remembered over and over in his mind, trying to pull them into a picture. He'd stalked around his small office, worked out, drank, and still the pieces didn't fit. Pete had done the same as Brett tried to focus on the detective's dilemma instead of his own. It hadn't worked.

Pete still stalked like a shadow through his mind, demanding Brett solve the mystery of the Vixen. He'd wanted to make her a villain, manipulating the detective's condition, but the threads wouldn't weave together. Still, it was clear she'd been hiding something even as the secrets of their bodies had been unmistakably exposed.

Brett was supposed to meet Sean tomorrow. He should call and cancel.

The more he puzzled over Allie, the less sense it made. She'd been wearing nothing but lingerie when she disappeared, and even that had been left behind. Had she shown up in someone else's home like she had in his? It didn't seem right. When she'd appeared in this room out of nowhere, she'd been wearing something, even if that something had soon somehow disappeared. She'd seemed sweet, uncalculating. Innocent. Could he really have been that wrong? Had it all been a scam she was now repeating elsewhere? Had she gotten whatever it was she had come for, or just decided they weren't the right target? Nothing was missing, though he'd obviously missed something.

As far as he could figure it, she had left naked and alone. Unless she'd had an accomplice waiting outside he hadn't heard. But he hadn't taken his eyes off her. He could have sworn she'd disappeared between blinks. That was too fast even for the best. Unless she'd drugged him, but of course he'd been the one to make breakfast.

He was going in circles.

Brett clenched his fists and forced himself to take a couple deep breaths. They didn't work, so he downed the scotch standing by his keyboard, ignoring the light burning in his throat.

He hadn't seen much of Vicky since Saturday, but he'd heard her moving around the house, so he knew she was okay. More okay than she would be if she ever saw him like this.

He had to get his act together. He had to get some work done.

He should probably take a shower.

He clicked open the drafts folder on his desktop. He hadn't touched it lately, working from the locked document. He scanned the old files, looking for something and nothing. An untitled one stalled his eyes, and he clicked on the file, opening the bottle of scotch and pouring one-handedly. He tipped the tumbler to his mouth before looking back at the screen.

Short lines of text, probably notes, covered part of the virtual page. Brett squinted so he could focus on the letters. He set down the scotch and shook his head. The poem was familiar, but it couldn't be his. He didn't write poetry. He checked the "created" date, but a little voice whispered he knew what he would find: the day Allie had arrived.

It is we: / The muses... For then you'd notice me / The muse who stands beside your chair...

Brett closed his eyes, willing the words to disappear. It wasn't possible.

Someday your eyes will clear / And you'll see me.

She had appeared out of nowhere and disappeared into nothing. She'd known he was a writer. She had literally inspired him. And Nate. And Vicky.

What if muses enhance the inclination to produce? The conversation wormed its way to the surface of his muddled thoughts.

Do you know something we don't? he'd asked her in the makeshift gallery. She'd only smiled in return.

But Vicky had seen it in Nate's painting. *Like you're the one who gave him his art.*

It was official: he'd lost his mind.

Allie had missed the calm beauty of her realm, though she had never felt quite so lonely wandering through it. Her favorite secluded pool had a clear waterfall that beat almost silently into the water. Large, flat stones lined the outer edge of the pool opposite the falls. Sunlight warmed them to a perfect temperature, but then most of faerie was idyllic. If she stepped into the water, her garment would dissipate into nothing more than a mist, to rematerialize effortlessly when she resurfaced, if she so desired.

Allie lowered onto a stone, dangling her feet in the water. Faerie stretched infinitely, so no one else ever came to this pool. No one had reason to deviate from a preferred haunt.

She pressed her hands into the smooth warmth below her and slid into the water, its depth ideally suited to her height. Had bathing also transitioned into fae culture from the mortal realm? It wasn't as though hygiene concerned them as it did the humans.

Allie lifted the spill of her hair, which dried instantly, and spun in the water with closed eyes. She had most missed the splendor surrounding her. She would become reaccustomed to the solitude. Or perhaps she could befriend Liliana, the sprite who had interfered on Allie's behalf and who had seemed not displeased to learn that Allie had returned.

A tiny figure greeted the reopening of her eyes. The water covered her, but Allie dropped her hair, which repositioned itself demurely. The scene almost echoed Nate's painting, except for her companion.

"Hello, Rizen."

The weaver fell into the water with a small splash and a resounding plop. Almost instantly, he reappeared seated on the stone, albeit wetter. Weavers' powers were limited outside the bounds of dreams, though the sunlight would dry his attire soon.

"Alexandra," he whispered, staring at her. "You see me?"

What a strange reaction. "Weavers aren't hidden from our sight."

"No." His features contorted bitterly. "But the *cursed* one is."

Chapter 23

Even the perplexing events of the last weeks couldn't have prepared her for that answer. Suddenly uncomfortable in the water, Allie transported herself, instantly clothed, to the shore. Walking out would have been no less demure, but it would have been much too reminiscent of Brett's comment at the art show.

Rizen scrambled to his feet. "Alexandra?!"

"I'm still here." His pain and panic were reasonable, if he truly was the cursed one, unseen and unfelt by both mortals and his own kind. He spun on the stone to face her. "No one speaks of the one who is cursed."

"Yet you know my tale."

"Only vaguely." The story had taken on many forms, as such were wont to do. He claimed to be the cautionary tale that prevented many from any temptation of crossing the Fates by breaking the rules. Curious, she settled on a stone beside his. "If you are cursed, why can I see you?"

"I could not say." His gaze never left her. "You were not intended to remember."

The details of the dream were fuzzy, but she was certain he had come to her. "Is this another mortal dream?"

"No." A parody of a smile twisted his lips. "But I know you wish it were."

She refused to consider the comment's ramifications. "Am I your loophole? A muse who saw you in a mortal dream?"

Rizen clenched his fists, but she knew he wouldn't leave. Centuries unseen, unheard, unfelt—a specter. Apart as Allie felt from her peers, they did acknowledge her presence.

"Is this what you do now? Observe us, unseen?"

"Don't you begrudge me my single pleasure!"

"I think I would prefer to be alone, away from those who cannot see me." In truth, she had grown to like being seen, particularly by Brett. Was Rizen her warning from the Fates?

"You're wrong." For the first time since she had noticed him, he looked away, over the water. "I thought I loved her, you know," he said eventually.

"The mortal?"

"She was incomparable. Her dream was pure happiness, and I couldn't resist. I joined her in the dream. Larger, of course. I took a human form." He sighed, closing his eyes. "We laughed, and played, and it was an easy joy. I made her happier that night than the man to whom the humans bound her ever could." He reopened his eyes but didn't look at Alexandra, though she could no longer glance away. This was the story whispered, dismissed, transformed, and feared, but it was more. She was the first, perhaps the only, creature who would hear it from the source.

"Occasionally, the humans remember dreams and want to repeat them. They need the same weaver for that, to rebuild the world they seek. She called to me, and I didn't think about refusing. We came together on the second night, and then the third. In dreams, I ensured she had an easier life than the burdens of the mortal realm, and I quickly grew to crave her company, her attentions, her unabashed affections.

"I recreated the dreams without her calling, drawing her into sleep and keeping her there, with me, for far too long. The humans called it 'sleeping sickness.' Her mortal body lost its luster without nutrition, activity, sunlight. But in her dreams, in my arms, she was vivacious, and sweet. Welcoming, and loving. And we were happy.

"The humans tried to wake her. Initially I would let them, but I despised the time apart, and she had grown weak. Weavers may shape the dreams, but it's the mortal's life that powers them. Her energy was never meant to sustain such extended forays into the crossover world, and she was lacking nourishment, but I was new and didn't know." He laughed bitterly. "I wouldn't have cared. I wanted her with me, seeing me, loving me. I didn't understand that dreams to mortals could never be anything more than a temporary escape, so soon I stopped letting the mortals draw her out.

"She dreamt of me and happiness as her mortal form wasted away, and I lost her to the human frailty."

Stillness met his silence, and Allie didn't move to break it.

He looked to her, and a centuries-old grief still tinged his gaze. "Thus I became the cursed one: unseen, unheard. Incapable of interacting with the fae and unremembered by humans if I ever joined their dreams, restricted to my true shape even then."

The lesson was unquestionable. "We are not intended to share the lives of mortals."

"I didn't share her life, Alexandra. I stole it." The confession tumbled out, as though he had waited centuries for a chance to share. Perhaps he had. "I stole her from her son, who watched her waste away as I took pleasure in her company, in her arms.

He dreamt of being held by her for years to come. She never had a choice."

Neither had Brett. Liliana had intervened soon after Allie's initial transformation. "I know my role and have resumed it." She could not comment on a heartbreak older than herself.

"Have you? Then who, pray tell, is your current charge?"

"You ask as though you know."

"You know as well as I that time flows differently for the humans. He does not write, and barely sleeps, not even dreaming, without you."

The pressure would be building inside him with no escape, tormenting him. "Could you go to him?" The question slipped out though she knew better than to ask.

"Oh, ho! And why would I do that?" The guarded Rizen had rebuilt, a shell around the wounded story, but Allie saw beyond it now.

"If I am the sole creature who can see you, I suppose we would become frequent companions."

"He does not need a weaver. He needs his muse."

"I cannot return to be unseen by him. Surely you of all understand that."

Rizen's eyes narrowed on her.

"He does not want me there," she finally confided.

"And how can you be certain?"

"He stated so, when I regained my form."

"Mortals! They know not what they need, and say not what they want. You could return and see the truth of his thoughts."

"How?"

"You are his muse," Rizen reminded, as though she had lost her wits.

He wasn't wrong. As his muse in truth she could once again hear his contemplations, so she could direct his work, nurturing promising seeds. "I am not certain what would be worse, learning he prefers me gone, or knowing he would want me there and yet remaining unable to join him."

"You can return to mortal form, Alexandra. Though you would have no loopholes a second time."

"I wouldn't expect such advice from you, of all creatures."

Rizen kicked his feet though they didn't reach the water. His clothing had already dried. "Don't you love him?"

"Irrelevant." Whatever her jumbled feelings meant, they could turn out to be nothing more than a residual effect of living as a mortal. "You thought you loved your mortal, yet wouldn't you now claim you had been wrong?"

"I was selfish. I plucked her from her life, loving her affection for an illusion, and allowing her to waste away."

"Yet counsel me to do the same."

"Think before you speak, Alexandra," he snapped, popping into an upright position so he could stalk about the stone below him. "With me, she was removed from life. You rejoined his, complementing it. You would share a life, built together with him, and he would know you for who you are." Pained eyes trained back on her. "Consider what you're passing up."

"He doesn't believe in muses," Allie stated, fighting the whirlwind of emotion the weaver's words stirred.

"And does your role define you? Is there nothing more beyond your function?" He paused, still staring at her. "I suppose it doesn't matter, does it? Either way you must return to your charge, to see beyond his words, or fulfill your role."

"And if he doesn't…" The thought held too much weight to finish.

"Love you back? Then you will learn bitterness. And then you will move on with poisoned memories, and you will do your *duty*." He spat the final word.

His anger prickled along her skin. The air had chilled in response, reacting to his emotions, though the rock beneath her remained warm. A realization fought its way from her subconscious. "If I returned to him, and if he wanted me, of which it is impossible to be certain, I could live a mortal life. I would not see you again." If she truly was the only one to see him, the weaver's very counsel was an inordinate sacrifice.

Rizen shook his head slowly. "I should not have to tell you that the briefest instant of love, real love, is worth more than an eternity without it."

Chapter 24

Brett's eyes burned, but he still stared at the screen. For Vicky's sake, he'd stopped drinking and even showered, but sleep still eluded him. So did his story. He'd decided the Vixen would be the mastermind, but his fingers refused to carry it through.

He'd rescheduled with Sean. Vicky claimed it was love-sickness. He'd told her he was over it, but she'd just snorted and rolled her eyes. She knew he'd been lying before he'd admitted it himself.

How had he gotten himself into this mess? He'd told Vicky he wouldn't stay single forever, but that was mostly for her sake. He wanted her to believe in the love their grandparents had had. Hell, maybe even their parents had had. They hadn't cared for their children, but they'd been a perversely good couple, suited to each other. Brett hadn't been interested in conning people, so they'd left him behind. Now he lied to people for a living, but at least they knew he was doing it.

But he didn't believe in happily ever after, not really. Some-where between raising Vicky and working his ass off for a semi-stable life, he'd realized perpetual bachelorhood suited him just fine, much better than being walked out on without warning. If he wanted love, he could always write it in his books. In the real world, he'd decided Vicky's happiness would be enough for him.

But now he wanted Allie back. She could be a mythical muse, or crazy, or maybe he was crazy, but it didn't matter, because he just wanted her. Her smile, the darkened passion of her eyes, the feel of her hair cascading over them when she was in his arms… Every cheesy cliché people wrote about two bodies being made for each other didn't seem so ridiculously farfetched anymore. She'd breathed new life into every part of his.

He missed her.

"People are replaceable," he'd once arrogantly claimed to his grandfather.

"Not the ones you love," the wiser man had answered instantly.

Brett had only seen the truth of that wisdom when his grandmother had passed. Soon after, her husband followed, wasting away from heartbreak. Brett was sure he couldn't know love like that, not after moving around so much that he'd never even learned to make friends—conning people into liking him was a different matter altogether.

But he hadn't conned Allie, maybe because she'd shown up so unexpectedly he hadn't been given a chance. She knew him, and Vicky had confessed that she'd shared the secret of their past, so she knew that too. He hadn't really thought about it with her there, but now he couldn't scrub the image of a future together from his mind. He wanted the chance to make her happy enough that she wouldn't want to leave, that she would think he was reason enough to stay. If there'd have been anywhere to start, he would've tried to track her down.

Vicky continued to claim she would come back. The miniscule part of him that still longed for love believed her. The rest of him knew better.

For the first time in days, he started to type. The tapping of the keys grew into a rhythm that pushed him forward. At least he could try to give Pete the happy ending he'd never get.

Magic protected her from discovery, but Allie still didn't dare move. The patchy sequence of a future together as Brett envisioned it had pierced through the muddled haze of her emotions. She wanted that future, infinitely more than a return to her own kind—the other fae who had barely seen her and never cared for her presence. Knowing Brett wanted her near made it impossible to consider returning to her realm, her duty, once his book was done and her assignment over. As a muse, she wouldn't be given much choice.

Was this love—the mutual desire to face a finite life together? What if she forsook her role, becoming mortal, only for him to reconsider? Rizen's bitterness wasn't incomprehensible. Although, a bitter mortal life sounded better than a heartbroken eternity.

The elderly couple she had once noticed in the diner flashed through her mind, and against all reason, the prospect of growing old and frail in mortal form, by Brett's side, became unbearably, inexpressibly tantalizing.

Brett paused in his work, twisting his head to stare at the spot where Allie stood. When his eyes couldn't find her, they drifted shut, and his shoulders hunched. Allie snatched her hand back before it could touch him of its own volition.

She bit her lip and called silently for Rizen, who appeared on the couch. The weaver looked to her charge, then back to her, before raising his hand in a silent farewell.

"Goodbye," Allie mouthed in return to this final representative of her realm. Rizen held her gaze for a prolonged moment, then disappeared. Allie blew her breath out, asking the Fates to redirect her course to mortal life.

Weight seeped through her body. Unlike the first transformation, mortal cloth appeared around her, as though a final sendoff from faerie. She swallowed roughly and debated how to approach the man who worked away.

He stilled, staring at the screen. Allie barely had a chance to glance at the shadowed reflection she now cast before he spun in the chair, shooting up and toward her. He stopped less than a weaver's height before her.

"Tell me you're real," his ragged voice whispered.

Allie nodded, but he didn't budge. "I'm real." *And human.*

As soon as the words were out, his hands were cupping her head, tilting it up for a kiss that dispelled most of her lingering anxiety.

He kept hold of her even when they finally broke for air. "Where were you?"

"You'll think I'm crazy."

His hands dropped to her shoulders, and he considered her as though untangling distant, transient threads. "You really are my muse."

Allie's fingers curled at their spot on his waist. "I used to be."

"And now?"

"And now I'm mortal. Human."

His fingers flexed gently into her. "Until?"

"Forever." Her voice caught on the word.

"Why?" he breathed, staring at her with increased intensity.

Allie licked her lips. *Moment of truth, Alexandra.* Too bad she could no longer hear his thoughts. "To be with you."

Brett didn't move.

Unwelcome tightness filled her chest, and she lowered her hands to her side, leaning away from him. "Unless you would rather—"

His fingers halted her backward movement. "Don't ever leave."

Air rushed out of her lungs in relief. One of his hands slid softly down her arm to tangle their fingers together as the other lifted to her cheek. His lips brushed hers, and Allie smiled at the gently thrilling pressure.

"I love you," he murmured against her mouth.

Allie pulled back to see him clearly. In this place, she had learned the transformative power of words, and she did not take them lightly. Finally certain of the truth, she watched joy light his eyes as she confessed, "I love you, too."

Epilogue

S o, what do you think?" Vicky asked, handing Brett a floral paper cup with some homemade lemonade.

"Not bad." He looped his free arm around her shoulders.

"The kids look like they're having fun."

"Yeah, that was a great idea."

Little ones colored copies of stylized flowers Vicky'd drawn, while the older ones twisted together flowers from tissue paper and pipe cleaner. Parents chattered in groups or helped their kids. A table stood with stacks of the picture book and piles of free bookmarks, all waiting to be signed. The Reading Corner had turned out to be a great place for their release party.

Vicky grinned. "Cheers."

Brett tapped his cup against hers, smiling back.

He still had a hard time believing this had all been worked out in several months. An independent press had offered him and Vicky a pretty solid contract, asking for only some minor changes to the text and none to the illustrations. Sean swore otherwise, but Brett was pretty sure it had something to do with his agent knowing the editor, especially after seeing the two of them observe the room together. They stood by the refreshment table, bodies angled toward each other, chatting easily.

Kristie and Nate had also shown up and even volunteered to help. The children kept them busy overseeing the crafts. Nate tucked a colorful paper bloom into Kristie's ponytail, and she giggled, leaning into him.

No one had paid much attention to the book itself yet, but everyone seemed to be enjoying the party, which was half the battle.

"Ladies and gentlemen, great and small!" Vicky's friend Jess called. Some giggling and shushing later, all eyes turned to her. "In just a moment, our incredibly talented authors will be happy to begin signing books and gifts for you."

Vicky elbowed him with a grin, and Brett obediently moved to their designated table.

"But first!" Jess continued, "Please welcome our extra-special guest, who has graciously taken a break from her many duties to spend the afternoon with all of you!" She tugged on a rope to pull the makeshift curtain behind her aside, revealing Allie.

Children squealed and rushed over. With the help of some parents, Jess wrangled them all into a mass mildly resembling a line. Brett had tried to warn Allie, but Vicky had convinced her to dress up in a gauzy dress, complemented by a floral wreath in her hair, and pose for photos with the kids. She answered questions about faerie and giggled with the children as parents snapped photos to take home and Jess took some promotional shots.

Vicky had also convinced Allie to model for some of the art classes, now that the new semester had started up, so she'd become more comfortable with the spotlight. She didn't seem to miss the invisibility. Whatever powers had brought them together, they'd also gifted her with a valid ID, not to mention Master's degrees in Art History and Comparative Literature. Now that she didn't try to hide her past from him, he was constantly astounded by the breadth of her knowledge.

She'd also decided to take a basic computer skills course, which was probably a good idea nowadays. Brett had tried teaching her, but they'd kept getting distracted.

Thankfully, she'd gotten even closer with Vicky since her return. Whenever the girls had a free moment, they slipped off to do one craft or another. The house had become cluttered with knickknacks. Vicky kept trying to convince him it was cozy. At the very least, it was nothing like their childhood—way too much stuff to ever pick up and move quickly, but that was a point in Vicky's favor. In any case, he definitely liked the crooked, clay pot Allie had made and filled with a small gardenia plant. She'd insisted it live in his office, to brighten up his workspace. Who was he to argue?

Brett's hand slipped into his pocket, ensuring the small velvet box hadn't disappeared.

"Are you excited?" Vicky murmured beside him.

"Of course. I'm thrilled this all seems to be working out."

She scrunched her nose. "I meant the ring."

Of course she had. Her keen eyes wouldn't have missed the anticipatory gesture.

A little girl in a pale-pink dress stepped nervously in front of his and Vicky's table, and Vicky fixed her with a friendly smile. "Hey, there."

The little girl looked to her mom, who nodded encouragingly. "Could I get a book, please?" she asked, gaze bouncing between him and Vicky.

"Well, sure!" Vicky pulled a book from the pile and flipped over to the title page. "I'll tell you what," she whispered conspiratorially. The little girl inched closer. "We'll even sign this book *and* a bookmark for you. Would you like that?"

The little girl grinned and nodded.

"What's your name?"

"Sandy." She stretched her neck to watch Vicky sign.

Brett glanced at his inspiration, catching her eye. Allie's expression sobered for a heartbeat before spreading into a more intimate smile. Mythical muse or no, he hoped she'd inspire him for life.

Another little girl, this one with frizzy pigtails, tugged on Allie's hand, reclaiming her attention. Vicky slid the book to him, and Brett uncapped his pen to sign below Allie's stylized portrait.

When Sandy walked away, book in hand, he turned back to his expectant sister. "Excited doesn't begin to cover it."

— Acknowledgments —

I owe effusive thanks to:

Rachel, who suffered through the very first (read: written in high school) version of this book and still volunteered to read the new one. I'm thrilled you've found your very own happily ever after!

Jillian, for her sharp eyes and endless encouragement;

Sinead Delaney, the writing teacher who plodded through the original version of this story and never once told me how horrible it truly was, or to give up;

the ladies of my writing group, for their unabashed and enthusiastic criticism;

and most of all my family, for their unflagging support through it all.

— About Aria —

Aria Glazki's first kiss technically came from a bear cub. Though no fairytale transformation followed, she still believes magic can happen when the right people come together—if they don't get in their own way, that is. So now Aria writes heartfelt romances about relatable people overcoming real-world obstacles to build love that lasts.

Aria Glazki
Relatable People — Remarkable Love
www.AriaGlazki.com